Professor Spindlebrock's

Lost Rognvald Scroll

Joseph D. Lyman

ISBN: 978-1-7363739-6-5

Typefaces: Libre Baskerville, by Rodrigo Fuenzalida, SIL Open Font License v1.1; Antique Book Cover, SIL Open Font License v1.1; Lime Glory, by FF user Lime; FFC License; Akura Popo, by Twincolabs Foundation, FFC License.

Images: Cover photography by Jason Leung, Grunter Tee, and Stephanie Lyman, Free Commercial Use Licenses; "Mystic Celtic Knot Flourish" a derived work from public domain vectors; All other images, modifications, and elements are original copyright works.

Pinpoint Management, LLC. Fulton, Missouri

To my mom,

who always believed in me.

CONTENTS

Chapter 1

A Promise From Spindlebrock

Looking back and writing about events—especially important ones—presents a unique challenge. Life happens like a whirlwind, with situations, people, and places all tossed about violently in a reckless and hastily put together performance. Nothing about it is sensical or organized, even when taken as a whole. Yet, we expect ourselves to be able to write about it in an organized, tempered, even-keeled fashion.

When I started the first part of these memoirs, in Professor Spindlebrock's Little Blue Book of Traveling Spells, I thought that sharing my tales would be simple. I recall sitting down to type page one, with a fresh feeling of optimism. Before the first keystroke was achieved, I imagined that I would be able to encompass all of the related memories in a single volume, with time and energy to spare. Writing about the abductions brought the rushing feeling of the whirlwind of life back in a way that I did not forecast, and the project naturally expanded as mental recall swelled and widened.

Now as I sit down to continue my account, I find myself apprehensive. You might think, reader, that having been introduced to magic and the magical commonality in the way that I was, and having worked directly on the Crane Abductions and other cases, I would be prepared for anything. But the depth of the information I intend yet to share, in this book and the next, fills me with apprehension.

Some of these revelations will shock both magician and non-magician alike; I'm not really sure which group will be more taken aback. Those who are not connected to the magical commonality don't have the benefit of context which many magicians will have as they read, the latter being unavoidably aware of the current state of affairs. Yet I am certain that both magician and non-magician will find interest and enlightenment in these pages.

One focus in what I have shared and will yet share, necessarily, is to impart to the reader certain facts pertaining to the elusive W.C. Crane, who played such a prominent role in my introduction into the magical commonality, and who has become somewhat of a legend in magical circles. His story intertwines with mine and Spindlebrock's in meaningful ways; and so, while those facts pertaining to him aren't the only important ones in my recollections, they are the main thread which I will pursue.

For that reason, I will forgo a long description of the Moquegua Forgeries, which rocked the magical world just nine short months after the abductions, and which many over the years have given me credit for solving. This was the case that originally made my gift of Conexus semi-public, at least to those who pay attention to such happenings. I'll also bypass the case of the Arson Triangle, about a year after that, which tried my very soul—and which Spindlebrock jokingly refers to as "Thomas Martin's Triumph," just to tease.

I bring these two cases up because it would seem odd, for some of my magician readers, for me to ignore such high-profile cases entirely. While they most certainly did happen, and I did play a part in them, they had nothing to do with W.C. Crane. Some believe—and Spindlebrock certainly played a part in overstating the facts—that I alone was to thank for their resolutions. Nothing could be further from the truth; no one truly works alone. Some day I may write more about them, but for now these two events may be set aside.

It was after the Arson Triangle that the now infamous theft of the Rognvald Scroll occurred. A recitation of the facts from my perspective might be confusing for those somewhat familiar with the incident, which was widely publicized; I do not apologize for the truth, but I give fair warning that this story might not be what you expect. All I can offer is my inside perspective, and additional insights and clarity on the scroll and Crane and all involved, which I'm certain will represent more than what is already generally known in the commonality.

I recall the events leading up to the theft quite well. Spindlebrock and I were playing an evening game of chess, when he brought up a subject that he had often used to torment me—speaking from my own perspective. At the risk of channeling his preachy tone, I'll share the relevant bit of our conversation here.

"So, have you changed your mind about God?"

His eyes remained fixed on the board.

"What? No. Why would I?"

"Perhaps you've gathered additional information, or had new experiences."

He moved his white bishop into position.

"I haven't. Have you changed your mind, and stopped believing?"

I moved my knight. Spindlebrock's focus remained solid, in spite of our chatter.

"No one has ever asked me that. Why should I do that?"

"Well, perhaps you've gathered additional information, or had—"

"Flippant rejoinders; are you trying to deflect?"

"I'm tired of you bringing it up, that's all."

"I see, but I wonder if you've considered that I might be purposefully obnoxious."

"Oh, I'm sure you are. But, you might try a more direct approach."

He moved his knight, threatening my queen and rook.

"I thought I was being direct. I ask simple questions, you give simple answers—"

I saved my queen; my rook fell.

"No, I mean, you might just say what you really want, what your obnoxious purpose actually is."

Spindlebrock moved his queen.

"I see. Check."

My knight stepped in to block.

"Really, now I want to know. What is your obnoxious purpose?"

"I would say that my purpose is to share. Over the course of my lifetime, I've discovered certain things, and have come to certain understandings and beliefs. I see value in those things, and wish to share them."

"So, you want to preach to me?"

My knight fell.

"Not in the slightest. I want to entice you. Check."

My king retreated. Spindlebrock followed.

"Entice me? Entice me to what end?"

"To explore. I ask if you believe, you tell me that you do not. Yet, I know you've done no research, no exploration, no work. You choose not to believe, with no real basis for your unbelief. I, on the other hand, have done a great deal of work. I see value in the work I have done, and what it has produced. I simply want to entice you to explore."

I gave up and moved my queen aimlessly to block. It would die, and the game would be lost. I wasn't in the mood for chess anyway.

"You know, I already study a great deal. I explore a great deal. I'm not convinced that what you suggest will be worth it."

"Have you known me to waste time or energy on meaningless pursuits?"

"Well..."

"Be fair. I study odd subjects, some in great depth, but I always have a purpose, an application."

"That's true."

"So, if I tell you that there is value in understanding God, would you at least explore the notion?"

"Perhaps. But how? Where would you have me start?"

"Never mind how, I leave that entirely up to you. Will you commit to some exploration of the subject? I'll promise to stop taunting you, and you can start feeling like you're on solid footing in your decision."

"I never felt that I wasn't," I lied.

Spindlebrock ignored the board and eyed me as I pondered his proposition for a few moments. The terms were quite reasonable, and a promise from Spindlebrock wasn't an everyday occurrence.

"Very well, I'll do it. I'll at least explore the notion, as you put it."

Spindlebrock took my queen, then gently pushed my king over with his piece. He leaned back and smiled.

"Checkmate; but, you weren't really trying."

"My head wasn't in the game today."

"I could tell. That's why I brought up God."

That was the last time Spindlebrock has ever initiated a discussion about my beliefs. If I broach the subject he's more than happy to talk, and we've certainly covered many related topics over the years; but since that day, it has always been on my terms.

Of course, owing to my nature I was quite concerned with the commitment I had made. I didn't exactly know where to start. I didn't feel like appealing to any of the usual sources; the Bible, priests, or the like. But I couldn't let it slide, and I really didn't want it sitting in the back of my mind.

Before I explain my attempted approach to this small problem, I should update readers on a particular individual who played a part in the abductions of my previous book;

Olivia Zhang. You may recall that in consequence of her involvement in the aforementioned affair, Olivia had been required to remain under the supervision of Dr. Patel while studying at the University of Magic, Toronto (where she had studied previously). While there, she made the most of her situation by applying herself fully to her studies. She became a fast favorite of every professor she studied under. Even Spindlebrock took to her again; though, he never quite forgave her handwriting.

Our paths crossed often, and in spite of our odd first introduction in Turkey, we eventually became friends. We had arranged to meet one afternoon between classes, for a late lunch. I arrived after she did, and from afar I noticed she was reading a small book. As I approached, she attempted to conceal the book under her papers, but when I reached the table, I quickly slid my hand in and snatched it up.

"Well now, what's this?"

"Hey! Give it back."

I could tell that she wasn't truly upset, and I was feeling playful, so I withheld it. Flipping the book over, I read the title and author aloud, "The Great Beyond, an Examination – Hamilton".

"It's nothing. Some light reading."

I flipped through, glancing at the pages.

"What's it about?"

"Your friend wouldn't approve."

I understood that she meant Spindlebrock. A page stood out to me, and I started to read aloud as I sat down.

"With all the preparations completed, I retired to the exact spot described in the ancient text. The celestial alignment was correct, including the lunar phase and all applicable bodies. Using the primary phase modulation method I have described, I made my first attempt..."

I flipped the book back over one more time and examined the cover again.

"Really, what is this?"

"If you must know, it's about ghosts."

An idea presented itself to me in that moment: Could this be my solution to Spindlebrock's little challenge?

"Ghosts? You mean dead people?"

"Spirits, astral beings, of the dead perhaps, or not. Definitions and terms vary. Not much is really known about them. I use the terms ghost and spirit interchangeably. "

"But, you think they might exist? Is this really just light reading?"

"Well, more of a hobby I guess."

Over lunch, I explained the commitment I had made to Spindlebrock. He wanted me to examine the possibility of a Supreme Being, I wasn't really interested. He told me I had done no work, I promised that I would.

"So, what do you think? Maybe I could piggy-pack on your hobby, and call it an investigation into theology?"

"It's a stretch. Plus, like I told you, he wouldn't approve."

"Well, we specifically agreed that I would do this my way —and this is my way. Tell me everything you know."

As it turned out, Olivia was quite versed on the subject. She had studied it extensively after an experience she had as a child. Her interest in elemental magic—which Spindlebrock once told me was one of her greatest strengths —stemmed from her interest in spiritual beings. Seeing that my enthusiasm was real, and being attuned to the subtle benefits of getting under the professor's skin a bit, she agreed to pull me in on her studies.

"All I ask," she said as we parted, "is that you let me see the look on his face when you tell him."

Chapter 2

How I Kept My End of the Deal

It was several weeks before professor Spindlebrock became informed of my new metaphysical pursuit. There had been no expectation of a timeline set in my commitment to "explore the notion of God," so I didn't feel any particular obligation to update the professor on the matter. In my heart I knew that Olivia was right, that he would not view the study of Ghosts as much of an inroad into theology. I dreaded telling him, and so I avoided the subject.

Summer was fast approaching. Olivia and I had been researching ghosts together for weeks during our spare time, mostly in quiet corners of the campus library. Desiring to make the most of the new warmth of the season, we decided to take a few books out to the commons, to soak up the rays while we read. Spindlebrock must have seen us from afar; he snuck up without either of us noticing. I was reading a passage out loud to Olivia, who was lying on a bench with her eyes closed. As I finished one account of a paranormal interaction, I was startled by the sudden intrusion of his authoritative voice.

"A shocking lack of fundamental data."

I jumped. Olivia opened her eyes and sat up.

"Sorry, I thought you saw me coming."

He knew that we had not seen him, but didn't wait for us to tell him so.

"I was just saying, that account really is lacking important information. May I see the volume?"

I handed him the book. He turned it over in his hands, then flipped through the front matter.

"Thought so. You'll never get anywhere with Clive, even as a co-author. You should be reading Burman."

Olivia chimed in.

"We've gone through Burman. Well, the three major works at least."

She glanced at me. I understood what she expected.

"Yes," I stammered, "we've been delving in quite deep, actually."

"Oh?"

"For weeks. I thought—I decided it would provide a good segue into my study of things spiritual."

He glanced at us both. Olivia tried to conceal a smile.

"Spiritual? As in literally, the study of spirits—or in this case, ghosts?"

"Sure," I ventured, "why not? People say God is a spirit. If I can prove spirits exist, it facilitates the proof of a God in some degree, right?"

"Your logic is faulty, but I see where you're coming from. Well, I guess it's a start."

He handed the book back. I was surprised that he didn't have more of a rebuke. Olivia appeared to be surprised as well. He turned and started to walk away, then paused and turned back.

"The thing is, you won't get very far in books alone. You'll want to experiment."

"Oh, I intend to," Olivia responded, "there are several promising venues that I've come across."

"Very good. And you, Thomas?"

"Well, we haven't talked about it much, but the thought had occurred to me."

I lied. In point of fact, the idea of hunting down ghosts chilled me. Olivia had brought it up, and was certainly planning on it, but I had never quite committed to the notion.

"Excellent. I have some experience with this sort of thing. If you're both interested, I can pull a few strings and get you lined up with a promising situation."

Feeling less and less comfortable, I grasped at the possibility of the professor's help and protection if such a venture were to come to fruition.

"Are ghosts something that interest you as well, that you would know of such an opportunity? Is this something you could show us, help us discover?"

Olivia, as fiercely independent as ever, scoffed faintly but audibly at my vague plea for his assistance. Spindlebrock walked back to us and sat down.

"At one point I had a great interest in the subject, Thomas. But, I've since moved on—to a degree. I can tell you both that you'll be embarking on a singular exploration, but that you'll inevitably find something other than what you seek. However, I certainly could not accompany you. I have more pressing matters to deal with. Plus, this is your journey."

He patted me on the shoulder.

"I won't interfere with your methods, even if I don't agree with them."

"But, you'll connect us with this situation?" Olivia implored.

"Absolutely. There is a place in India, where a ghost has been seen with some frequency for over a hundred years. The locale is a bit absurd in some ways, but the sightings are in fact real. I have some regular business there, I could arrange for free accommodation."

Olivia looked as if she were trying to remember something for a moment.

"Wait, India? I haven't studied much about paranormal activity there, but there was this one story—You're not talking about the Cascabela, are you?"

"You've heard of it! Yes, the Black Cascabela Museum—"

Olivia laughed scornfully.

"Museum? It's a casino with a vault that people can visit, not a museum. Are you trying to be funny, Professor? We're serious here. You may not put much stock in this, but we're making a thoughtful study. Carnival sideshows aren't going to help us."

"Now, now, Olivia, you're not being reasonable. You say it's a sideshow, I say it's real. What is your basis?"

"Well, for one, the Cascabela is an undisguised tourist trap. These people profit off of fraudulent paranormal tourism; it's their business model! They literally advertise a haunted tour, where you're guaranteed to see a ghost."

"Fair point. But, I'm not suggesting that you take the haunted tour, I'm telling you that there is a real opportunity in that place—"

"Really? And what's your basis for such a claim."

"Personal experience and a great deal of study."

Olivia was shocked. She opened her mouth once or twice, but found no words.

"Yes, Olivia, I have in fact seen the ghost that is there."

"I'm sorry, I—I didn't know."

Her demeanor changed entirely, and excitement entered her voice as she began to comprehend.

"You've seen one too? And you'll show us, point us in the right direction?"

"I will."

"What do you know about this spirit? Do you know their name? Did you communicate?"

Spindlebrock stood up. I thought I detected a faint look of satisfaction on his face.

"Why don't you and Thomas come with me to my office, and I'll tell you some of what I know, including enough information to hopefully get you on the right track."

Olivia was anxious to follow him, and so she did. I followed her, but as an unwilling captive, a victim of my own big mouth.

In the privacy of his office, we were informed that the ghost's name in life was Daksh Parikh. Spindlebrock had apparently studied the case in some detail. Daksh was supposed by many to have lived a couple of hundred years ago. The legend was that he had died in an accident, shortly after falling in love with a young woman whom he could not marry. His thwarted love and the mistreatment he received from the girl's father caused him such torment that he haunted the man, forcing him to leave India.

The professor was unwilling to describe his personal encounters with Daksh, though he adamantly affirmed that they were entirely real, and even reproducible. Rather than divulge details of his encounter—which would certainly influence our experience—he wanted us to discover him on our own with only the help we absolutely required, so that we could form our own ideas. To that end, he immediately made good on his offer to help us with free accommodations, by putting in a call to the casino and arranging our stay right there and then. Knowing that I was strapped for cash now that my student loans were in repayment, he even offered to let us use his frequent flyer miles to cover the cost of the flight. He would settle everything, and we would leave in a few weeks.

After she thanked him profusely, Olivia left in a hurry, anxious to prepare. I remained in my chair, my head swimming with the rapidity of this development.

"I'm sorry, Thomas, I think I owe you an apology."

"What? What for?"

"You clearly aren't as ready for this step as Olivia is."

He was right, but I dismissed his concerns and thanked him for his generosity. While I was indeed not prepared to move forward at such a pace, I was determined to make good on my commitment to study the Infinite. Furthermore, I was genuinely surprised and pleased to find Spindlebrock receptive of my chosen path. I would make the most of the experience, and enjoy some free travel while I was at it, even if it meant potentially getting a little closer than I liked to the stark realities of the universe and the people and things in it.

Chapter 3

Not on Our Itinerary

Neither Olivia nor I was nervous about international travel; in an irregular sense, we had already traveled abroad together. We spent the weeks leading up to our trip studying sightings in southern India (where the Cascabela is located), and trying to find out what we could about Daksh Parikh. As it happened, Daksh was barely a footnote in the complex paranormal history of the region, and Spindlebrock was suddenly too busy with what he called a "massive development" to enlighten us much further. His only response was a promise that he would "put us in possession of the pertinent information about Daksh, when it was most timely."

The day of our trip arrived, and our voyage started out smoothly. We were to fly from Toronto to Newark, Newark to New Delhi, and then on to Chennai, where we would travel by car to the Cascabela. Newark is under two hours on a commercial flight, hardly enough time to get settled and have a conversation; we completed the first leg without so much as a hiccup of turbulence. In fact, the only thing that went wrong was that I neglected to make a student loan payment before I left, so I had to make it from my phone while we were boarding our next flight.

As our plane was taxiing for takeoff to New Delhi, and before I remembered to put my phone back in airplane mode, a call came through. The flight attendant gave me a dirty look, but I answered it anyway; it was Spindlebrock.

"Thomas, have you left Newark yet?"

He was agitated. I tried to whisper, so as not to draw attention to myself.

"We're just taking off."

"Blast! Well, I guess I'll have to meet you there."

"What? What do you mean? Is everything alright?"

Olivia, who had been fiddling with an audiobook, pulled out an earbud and leaned in.

"Alright? It's an upheaval! But, there's nothing you can do about it from where you sit."

"What happened?"

"There's been a burglary. Something of great value."

I breathed a sigh of relief; no one I cared about was in trouble.

"Is that all? Look, I'll call you when we land in New Delhi. The attendant is coming this way."

"No, wait, this is important. I'm in the Gulfstream, already in the air. I'll meet you in New Delhi. Call me."

With that he hung up, just in time to keep me from getting in trouble with the flight crew.

"What was that about?" Olivia asked.

"It was Spindlebrock, something about a burglary. Apparently it was something big, he wants to meet us in New Delhi."

"Are you serious? And you want to wait for him there?"

"Well, he is paying for our trip."

The more than thirteen hour flight felt like an eternity, as I pondered on what could be so valuable that Spindlebrock would ditch his so-called "massive development" to investigate. Olivia, indefatigably studious, distracted me with quotes from a book she was working through on the subject of magically-enhanced spiritual encounters. Even so, time and clouds passed slowly.

After finally landing, deplaning, and locating our luggage, I was about to call Spindlebrock when I spotted a driver near the exit holding up a hand-scrawled sign that read "TOMUS MARTEN." He eagerly escorted us to his cab, in which Spindlebrock was occupying the front seat.

"Hop in, quick!"

We did as he said, and the cab sped off, tires squealing. I knew better than to start a conversation when the professor was in that kind of a hurry, but Olivia was less familiar with the man.

"What in the world is going on that requires that we drive like the earth is opening up behind us?"

Spindlebrock laughed.

"We have a party to get to—now, sit tight, I'll explain everything on the jet."

"What? We just landed!"

He had no reply. Our cab ride was a short one, to a private hangar off the Indira Gandhi International Airport access road. He paid the driver generously and we got out. We followed him through the hangar and to the tarmac, where the familiar Gulfstream G650 was waiting, refueled and ready for takeoff.

"Ugh—so this is how you got here before us. I should have guessed."

Olivia stopped in her tracks, apparently repulsed by the memory of the last time she had seen that plane.

"Private travel in a fast jet always beats commercial times—and I left before you did. Come, come! Not a moment to lose, you two!"

It was already dark. Spindlebrock kept checking his watch as we boarded, situated ourselves, and took off.

"This will be a short flight, and an even shorter drive than the one you had originally planned from Chennai."

"But, long enough to explain what's going on?" I asked.

"Certainly long enough for that."

"And after we're done with your little task," Olivia chimed in, "you'll get us to the Cascabela, so we can do the research we came here for?"

"We're heading there now, in point of fact."

"What?" Olivia and I responded in unison.

"The Black Cascabela Museum boasts one of the most secure magical vaults in the commonality. What you see as a tourist trap, those with rare and valuable goods see as a haven. This morning, just before you landed in Newark, an object was discovered to have been stolen from the vault's innermost chamber. The stolen object is of significant magical, scientific, and historical value; it was the Rognvald Scroll."

Olivia gasped audibly. At that time, I was unfamiliar with the Rognvald Scroll, so I interrupted and asked for more details. It was Olivia who responded.

"The Rognvald Scroll—also called the Kingmaker Scroll —is a relic that was created by Rognvald Eysteinsson, a powerful magician, in his final days at Giske, in ninth or tenth century Norway."

"I'm impressed," Spindlebrock responded, "you know your history. What else can you tell us about the scroll?"

"There's nothing else to tell. It's believed that Rognvald was working on some magic to concentrate power, to cement his bloodline as kings, but he was killed—burned alive in his home, with sixty of his most loyal followers—before he could complete his work. The scroll was salvaged from his burned-down home, and has been a valuable object of curiosity ever since. What I read last was that it was sold at auction for a ridiculous sum."

"That is close, and certainly all you'd get from any modern source on the subject. Allow me to clarify a few points for you both. Rognvald was not burned alive in an ambush, as is commonly recounted; his home was attacked, and he was interrogated. It was his refusal to hand over the scroll that led to his death, and the burning of his home and kin. The scroll was not salvaged from the wreckage, it was saved by Rognvald's most trusted apprentice, Mattis, who alone had been entrusted with the task from Rognvald himself.

"The continued existence of the scroll was known only to this apprentice for a number of years. He had assumed a new identify, and was not a figure in the magical world at all, until an accidental slip up which involved a young woman who was to become the most prominent magician of her generation. They fell in love, and the scroll was revealed to her. It was she who decided that the scroll was too important to keep a secret.

"Now, you said that the scroll was part of a study into the concentration of power. That is partially correct, but only in an objective sense; the scroll was part of something which might be used to help one gain and keep power, perhaps. The real purpose of the scroll was a study in the prolonging of life.

"To abbreviate the story, the woman betrayed the trust of her lover. He was marked as a target for a variety of power hungry magicians, who banded together with the sole purpose of discovering the scroll—"

"Please don't say you mean the Pyre Reich..." Olivia interrupted.

"You've connected the dots; that secret organization is the very one that forced Mattis back into hiding, never to be heard from again."

"This is worse than a cheap ghost story. The Pyre are practically mythology, Celtic treasure hunters, fabled to be seekers of the Fountain of Youth, or some such nonsense. I can see how one might try to connect the two tales, but really? And, even if all this were true, how would you know about it?"

"The rest of the story will answer that question. Mattis fled once again, and once again assumed a new identity. As he grew in power, he eventually took on an apprentice of his own, and work on the scroll continued. The scroll was passed down that way, from owner to apprentice, for more than a thousand years.

"Of course, in that amount of time even the simplest of facts—if interesting enough—warp into legends. But, to those working on it, the scroll was never more than an academic pursuit. Whether any amount of success was ever achieved related to the scroll's original intent, I cannot tell you. What I can say is, the scroll eventually gained the status of a valuable and unique curiosity—as you stated, Olivia. It was purchased by a collector many years ago, and has been on display at the Black Cascabela Museum in the secure inner vault ever since."

"That doesn't tell us how you know so much about it," Olivia noted.

"You are impatient. The scroll, you see, came with a variety of additional notes, including the history of the scroll's owners, and their understanding of it. That is where the somewhat private information I have just shared comes from—"

"Still don't know how you have that information," Olivia interrupted again.

Spindlebrock sighed.

"The scroll belongs the owner of this jet."

He motioned to the cabin as he spoke.

"Lucas Brevig, a collector, and a powerful magician."

"The Norwegian fellow?" I asked.

"Well, he has a home in Norway, but he's not Norwegian. Yes, that's the one."

Olivia looked thoughtful.

"You see," continued Spindlebrock, "I manage many of Brevig's affairs. This jet, some of his research—and yes, I am even tasked with protecting some of his most valuable collectibles."

We sat in silence for a few moments, taking it all in.

"So," Olivia said, "he pays you to make sure his collectibles are safe?"

"In a way. Primarily, we are academic associates. But, my pursuits take me out into the world more than his do, so I often act as his 'feet on the ground' in matters of management. I selected the Cascabela as a home for the Rognvald Scroll, for example. I even helped design and build the display."

At that point I realized why he was in such a dither: his own security measures had failed, and a priceless relic that was entrusted to his care was now missing. I immediately felt a surge of interest in the case, and a desire to reach out and offer my assistance in any way possible. But, Olivia— who had really only interacted with the professor as a student, and who viewed him as a meddler more than anything else—spoke up before I could interject.

"We've been studying and planning this trip for weeks. I have my own personal reasons that make this a very important trip for me, and Thomas is on a theological research errand that you put him up to. What good could we possibly be to the illustrious C.C. Spindlebrock?"

Spindlebrock laughed.

"You do know that the young man sitting next to you is arguably the most sought after forensic specialist in the magical commonality, do you not?"

He was speaking primarily of the resultant reputation that came from the two cases I mentioned at the beginning of this book. Olivia, of course, was aware of how uncomfortable I felt about my involvement, and the subsequent attention that Spindlebrock had directed my way. She had absolutely no problem speaking her mind on the subject.

"Thomas views the outcomes of those events rather differently than you do."

He raised his eyebrows. I decided to speak up before things got more awkward than they already were.

"Look, I have to confess that this case with the scroll— Rogenveil? How do you say it?"

Spindlebrock and Olivia both corrected my pronunciation in stereo.

"Thank you both—the Rognvald Scroll—I find it fascinating. Moreover, I'm dying to know how someone could break into any display you designed!"

Olivia rolled her eyes.

"Now, granted, we did come to India for a purpose. But, I see no reason we couldn't carry on with our paranormal investigations, and make room to help with this investigation as well, right?"

Spindlebrock elbowed my arm.

"That's the spirit! I don't want to ruin your investigations; in fact, I want to help them however I might. All I'm asking for is an expert opinion on this theft. You'll have more than enough time to do what you came to do."

With a few more words, it was settled. Shortly after takeoff, it seemed, we were landing at the Salem municipal airport near the Cascabela, and in a blur of a cab ride, we had arrived at our destination.

Chapter 4

The Cascabela

You have likely seen a casino, and so you probably already know that they are generally gaudy, pretentious, and veneered. They're designed to mobilize basic instincts, suggest the opulence that you might attain therein, and broadly appeal to anyone who has (or will shortly have) a few drinks in their belly. Not being a fan of psychological manipulation—and not having a desire to burn money frivolously—they hold no appeal for me.

At first glance, the Cascabela hits the mark for everything one might expect from a casino. Located in a mountainous forest northeast of Salem, you see hints of the building's impressive lighting as you approach from the winding, wooded avenue. The exterior theme is dark, to the degree that the building appears to be solid onyx black when approached at night, with highlights of deep purple, which are accentuated by recessed neon lighting. The glow through the trees is uncanny, but once the building comes into view, it morphs comfortably from eerie to elegant.

Architecturally, I would say the structure hints at New Brutalism, with hard lines and angles, and what I've heard described as "emphatic permanence." Part of the effect comes from the fact that the building is comprised of an original portion with eclectic yet stubbornly boxy additions, carefully added over time. The new portions are joined in such a way to make the whole look modern, almost angularly austere. If its architecture could speak, it would say to the traveler, "make haste, and enter."

A closer examination reveals that the original portion of the Cascabela must be as old as India itself. The entrance and the main hall are all that authentically remain; though they've been adorned to suit the building's modern purposes, their antiquity is difficult to mask. I've yet to discover for myself exactly when the original edifice sprung up, from whence it sprung, or why.

My descriptions, it should be noted, don't come solely from my first impressions of the building the night Spindlebrock, Olivia, and I arrived there. When our cab came to a halt in front of the entrance, I was exhausted, and wanted nothing more than to check in and find my pillow. To my tired eyes, the casino appeared only as a vaguely interesting sanctum for the proverbial fool and his money.

Originally, Olivia and I were to have our own adjoining rooms. Of course, with three of us arriving, Spindlebrock would share my room (we usually share a room while on a case, to give us a place to discuss details in private). As tired as I was, I refused his invitation to address anything related to the burglary that night. Informing me that he would be back up to the room as soon as he had checked in with the casino's proprietor, Spindlebrock went on his way, while Olivia and I retired.

In the morning it was apparent that Spindlebrock hadn't slept in his bed. He met up with us at breakfast.

"Good morning! And how are my two favorite ghost hunters this fine day?"

Olivia was chewing her food, and only nodded.

"I'm well enough," I responded. "How are you? You look unusually chipper—did you sleep well?"

"Sleep? Not at all. I was far too busy. After I met with Lowen, we determined that no time should be wasted in starting the full investigation. I've been up all night, surveying the grounds and the crime scene with him."

"Lowen is the owner?" Olivia asked.

"Yes, Lowen Walker. I thought you both knew that."

Spindlebrock looked back and forth between us.

"I've never heard of him," I said.

Olivia shook her head.

"Lowen Walker is the heir of an entertainment dynasty, a network of hotels, casinos, cruise ships and the like, that spans the globe. The Walkers are a famous magical family going back centuries, with destinations for the magically inclined on every continent. How could you not know the Walkers?"

"We've been busy paying for university," Olivia remarked, "not cruising the seven seas."

"I see your point. Well, Lowen was the only son of Adair and David Walker. He inherited the family businesses, legacy, and fortune about nine years ago when his father passed. He flew in as soon as he heard about the burglary. I'm sure you'll get a chance to meet him."

"What did you find? In your investigation, I mean," I asked.

"Well, to be honest, we spent the bulk of our time reviewing all of the many security measures that would have to be breached in order for the burglar to succeed. The moment I heard that a successful attempt had been made, I knew we were dealing with a professional, skilled in the utmost—an artist. I'm even more convinced now."

"So, you found nothing then?"

"We found very little. However, Thomas, I'd really prefer to let you draw your own conclusions. When you're done eating, meet me in the lobby, and I'll take you on the same tour that Lowen gave me."

"What about me?"

Spindlebrock smiled broadly at Olivia.

"You're more than welcome to join us."

"I don't really care about your investigations, you know that. I'm here to—"

"Yes, yes, I know. I only wanted you to feel welcome, that's all. In consideration of your purposes for being in India, I've arranged a special meeting for you."

"A meeting? With whom?"

"A friend, and a local expert in all things ghostly—and much more. He lives in Sathyamangalam, about a three-hour drive west of here. You'll be gone most of the day, but I promise it will be well worth your time."

Olivia was not excited about the idea of a long drive, but she thanked Spindlebrock for thinking of her and agreed to the plan. The professor left to arrange a cab while we ate.

"So, Thomas, you came all the way to India to pursue your spiritual study, only to get caught up in yet another investigation?"

I drank some juice to clear my throat.

"Believe me, I'm not anxious to waste my whole trip on a burglary."

"Liar. I could see it on your face when Spindlebrock mentioned the work of an artist."

I paused to consider the possibility that the case interested me more than I consciously realized.

"Maybe you have something there—but, if this crime was as elaborate as he makes it sound, then I doubt there is much we can do besides informing the insurance companies that they've got some payments to make."

After breakfast, we rejoined Spindlebrock in the lobby. A car was ready for Olivia, the driver paid for the whole day. We made sure she had everything she needed, and saw her off. Spindlebrock waited until her cab was out of sight before speaking.

"Right. Now everyone's happy. She absolutely will not be disappointed, and I pray we'll have equal success. Come, let us begin!"

Without another word, Spindlebrock turned and started for the parking lot on the south side of the building. I followed, knowing better than to bother asking where we were heading. Once we got to the edge of the parking lot, near the entry drive, we stopped and turned to face the building.

"OK, Thomas, here's where we'll start."

I glanced around idly.

"Hadn't we better start with the security camera footage?" I suggested.

"Yes, well, that's precisely where Lowen and I started last night. It led us here, and didn't give us much else."

Spindlebrock pointed to the casino.

"There, on the right side of that portion that juts out from the main building—you see that small squarish structure—that is where the burglar entered."

His finger followed a line from the part he was indicating, down the side of the building, and along a wall extending from the building to the woods.

"From the woods, they crawled along the top of the wall."

"Didn't the surveillance guards see him?"

"Him or her, Thomas, we don't know. No, they didn't see the burglar on the wall that night; Lowen interviewed them all. You can see the intruder on the footage, but only just and only if you're really looking. The cameras all focus primarily on the driveway and parking lot; that wall cuts the front of the property off from the back, and that side of the building is primarily for HVAC and property maintenance. It gets swept by the regular patrol, but in the surveillance room they apparently never see activity there, and tend to overlook it."

We started walking toward the woods on the side in question.

"The wall meets the woods at a small hill. You'll see that it would be quite a simple thing to get to the top. Crawling across it would be a different matter."

"Indeed," I said as we reached the wall, "I fail to see how an average person could get across the full length of this wall—it's incredibly narrow."

"Even so, they did, and with great speed and very little extraneous movement. They were agile."

"And small framed, I would guess."

"That's right. From the footage, I'd say maybe one sixty-five in height, and not much in bulk either."

I quickly converted centimeters in my head to five feet, five inches in height. For some things, I still can't get metric to sit right.

"I'm tempted to try it," I said, "but I don't think I'd make it all the way."

"The surveillance guards would have a good laugh—they're watching this area more closely now. Instead, let's head over to the main building. There's a ladder waiting for us—it was placed by the staff for Lowen and I, and I had them leave it up—so we can at least get a feel for the next little challenge that this agile creature had to conquer."

The wall connected to the main building in a nook behind a corner, and a tall ladder was propped up expectantly, a security guard posted near its base. I had to lean my head back to see the top.

"That wouldn't be a pretty picture, if one fell from up there."

"No, it would not. Now, how would you like to climb up? Your young legs are better suited to such tasks, and I've already had a rickety go at it with Lowen."

Heights were never my favorite thing after Adana, but with curiosity as my fuel, I started the climb. The ladder took me all the way to a small landing, which I clamored onto gratefully. Aside from pipes and HVAC equipment, there was a door and some space to stand, but nothing else. Looking down, I could see that the wall was a good two and a half yards below where I stood.

Spindlebrock shouted up to me.

"I'll go around from the inside, and meet you at the door."

I waved my understanding. As I waited, I tried to figure how one might make it from the wall to the landing. When he finally arrived, the professor knocked gently on the door before opening it.

"I didn't want to knock you off the ledge," he said, "there isn't a whole lot of room here. So, what do you think?"

"Does the security footage show them climbing up here?"

"Well, you can just see them on the landing for a moment before they go in this door, but from the angle of the camera, you can't actually see into the nook where you climbed up the ladder."

"It sounds like they're at least identifying some weak spots in their perimeter, out of all this."

"Indeed. Lowen was quite apologetic. They're having additional cameras installed this week, in fact. And, more locks."

Spindlebrock motioned to the door. The metal handle was old and rusted.

"Apparently, the only people that use this door are repairmen. It's never locked."

I laughed dryly.

"Are you serious?"

"That's exactly what I said. Come in here, and I'll show you the justification I received."

We entered the building. The air was hot, and the long, narrow room was poorly lit. Pipes and duct work forced us to squat a bit as we walked.

"There are two doors, on either end of this room. It forms a sort of hallway really, an access space. The air conditioning equipment enters the building here; this little room is only used for maintenance."

Spindlebrock made his way to one of the doors.

"Look—the locks on both doors are quite solid, and they're hinged on the other side. And, you'll note that the entry is keyed electronically, so anyone opening this door would trigger an alarm in security."

"Ah, so the exterior door wasn't of much concern, because it's too high to reach without a ladder, and actual building access is restricted once you're in this room."

"Precisely."

We walked back and opened the exterior door once more. The handle didn't even turn, it was so rusted; the door just popped open.

"But, apparently someone could reach this. What do you think, Thomas? How did they climb up?"

"Well, I was looking at that before you got up here. There isn't anything that they could have hooked with a grapple, and I see no evidence of marring on any surfaces that would suggest they tried. There's not much to climb, only some conduit, which certainly isn't secure enough even to hold a very light person's weight. Wait—what about that?"

On the other side of the conduit, where two concrete walls joined, was an expansion joint.

"That gap, see it? There, where the two slabs of this concrete wall meet. It's within reach of the platform."

I got on my knees and carefully stretched as far as I could to examine the joint.

"Ah! See there, bits of black lint, scraped onto the concrete. Someone has had a gloved hand jammed in there, and hard."

"Very good, Thomas! So, they used the joint like a rock climber would use a hand jam?"

"Looks like it," I said, standing back up. "They probably used the conduit as a counter, and the hand jam to help support their weight. They could have placed their feet against the edge of the nook there too, for extra support."

"Exceptional. We were stumped as to how they did it."

"Well, it would be hard to see the bits of black cloth, out here at night like you guys were."

"I wouldn't have thought to look that closely, or in that location. So, they climbed up that way, and we saw them as they stood, just before entering the building."

"Sounds like. Out of curiosity, how long was it on the video between the time you saw them on the top of the wall, and here on the platform?"

"That's the thing, they made very short work of it. I had speculated that they already had a rope or something placed, let down from the top, and that they took it with them."

"Even that would be difficult and take some time. Either way, it sounds like they're physically fit."

I started painting a mental picture of this burglar as we re-entered the maintenance room. We stood for a few moments, apparently both lost in thought.

"So," I continued, "how did they get into the building from here? The two doors were locked, and there was no indication that they were somehow opened?"

"None. We reviewed the video footage from the hallway cameras, in fact. The last time those doors were opened before that night was on a routine security check, about a week prior."

"And the ducts?"

"Not a chance. For one, they're too small. But even if someone managed to somehow squeeze through them, the ducts are equipped with vibration sensors—any movement beyond tolerance, and they'd be set off."

"Really? That's more advanced than I would have thought, given what we've seen so far."

"Well, don't judge too harshly. We're examining the weakest points of the Cascabela here, having already been shown where to find them through the actions a burglar who has clearly made a study of the problem."

"Yes, I suppose that is fair."

"Lowen has made some serious improvements since he took ownership a few years back. The hotel is well staffed, and the security for the most part is pretty tight. The perimeter needs more work, granted, and I'm sure that will be dealt with. What we need to know is, where did the burglar go next?"

No possibilities presented themselves. I looked around for some time before giving up.

"I just don't see how this burglar got into the building. If through the vents, they would have been detected. If through the doors, they would be on the camera footage. There's no evidence of either. I'm at a loss."

"Not to worry, Thomas. We were at a complete loss as well. We really have no idea how they got from this room to the vault. Let's set this challenge aside for a bit—let it marinate, so to speak. We'll skip ahead to where we know the trail resumes: the inner vault."

Chapter 5

An Impossible Crime

There's only one way to get to the museum—or vaults, as they're more often referred to—of the Cascabela. You must enter the main lobby, pass through the cavernous corridor which opens into the gambling hall, make your way through a maze of busy gaming tables, and approach the vaults through their one and only entrance; a large floor-to-ceiling gap in the massive concrete wall, flanked by two security cabins and a wide, complex series of three-arm turnstile gates.

Spindlebrock explained the wisdom and planning behind the building of the vaults as we wended our way quickly through this obviously security-centric pathway. As we arrived at the vault entrance, two guards stood ready to escort us in. A sign in front of the turnstiles that read, "Closed for Renovations" in multiple languages, was moved aside as we entered.

"You see, Thomas, this is the only way in or out, and it is heavily guarded."

"The only designated way in or out, you mean."

"Ah, true. Yes, we certainly shouldn't assume anything. Now, look here—"

We had entered the first exhibit hall. Two guards accompanied us, but gave us a very respectful distance, staying several yards behind so that we could work. The room was curved, and disappeared around corners on either side.

"The vaults are round in design. Each hall contains exhibits on either side of the aisle, as you walk around the circle. You must walk all the way around to the back, in order to enter the next hall, and each hall has a three-arm turnstile that you must pass through before entering—a magical turnstile, mind you. There's no jumping over it."

"Clever—so there is no quick exit."

"Quite right. The deeper you go into the vaults, the harder it is to get out quickly."

The guards followed as we slowly meandered around the first hall. I took my time, glancing at some of the relics, but mostly looking for hidden features of the building.

"The cameras are placed a bit high," I noted, "maybe a foot or two below the ceiling, but they're abundant. I imagine they cover the vaults very well from that angle."

"For the most part, and in these outer vaults, yes."

"The duct work is more narrow than usual. I see ventilation and return work, but nothing a person could fit into."

"Yes, they opted for more numerous small ducts, versus the more cost-efficient larger style. I've seen the plans, long ago."

I frowned.

"Well, you could have mentioned that."

"It was so long ago. The only thing I recall was that the walls were thick, heavily reinforced to leave no room for crawlspaces or large ducts. Lowen's parents designed it, they showed me the designs when I first came inquiring on Brevig's behalf."

"So, we really can rule out the ducts."

"I think so, but we're not assuming anything."

I conceded, and we continued our walk. Another turnstile, again flanked with guard cabins, led into the second, and another into the third vaults. Aside from some remarkable exhibits that I determined I'd have to spend real time examining some day, the building was uniform and solid. There were no emergency doors, or other obvious alternative pathways that a burglar might use.

"What about the floors?" I ventured, as we wandered through the much smaller third vault. "The carpet is plush, are we on concrete, or is there a basement?"

"Lowen said that the vaults sit on a concrete slab over an old granite foundation. No basement in this part of the casino. No way in through the ground, not without blasting or heavy equipment."

"And the ceiling? What is above us?"

We both looked up. The high ceiling helped the increasingly smaller vaults to feel less claustrophobic, but we could easily tell that the rooms were capped with concrete and steel.

"No, I can't imagine there is anything in that. I suppose we could go on the roof though, just to be sure."

As we approached the innermost vault, I noted that the entrance was a more narrow gap, still imposing from floor to ceiling, with a single guard cabin and a one-person turnstile. At this point, the guards that had led us into the vaults stayed back, and the single guard from the cabin led us into the innermost chamber.

"And here we are. One way in, one way out. Minimal vents, and a very small chamber."

I examined the inner vault. It was cylindrical, approximately eight yards in diameter. The showiness and décor of the outer vaults was abandoned; the inner vault featured bare concrete walls, a stained concrete floor, and minimal lighting. There were only a handful of exhibits here, mostly around the perimeter of the room.

Spindlebrock motioned to the center of the vault. There, in the middle of the room, stood a round exhibit, less than a yard in diameter, surrounded by red velvet ropes. The base appeared to be of solid brass. Atop the base there was a heavy glass tube, topped with a thick brass disc.

Inside the glass, sitting on a stand of red velvet, stood a most curious object.

"Is this it then?"

"This is it."

I approached, enthralled.

"What am I looking at? You said it was stolen."

"The scroll was stolen. What you're looking at is the scroll case."

Looking closely, I noted that the scroll case was not modern.

"How old is it?"

"While the Scroll of Rognvald dates to somewhere in the ninth century, the scroll case dates much further back. My best estimate is the late northern European Bronze Age, around six hundred BC."

"Incredible! It's perfectly preserved!"

"All signs would indicate that it has been carefully guarded throughout history."

"Even so, to survive for that long—"

I walked around the exhibit, examining the scroll case. It was bronze, about eighteen inches tall, and about the diameter of a grapefruit. It appeared to be comprised of a series of stacking disks, each with a collection of runes scrawled at very regular intervals. I noticed an opening at the top. It was ajar.

I stepped back, and began to examine the display enclosure.

"So, they got in there somehow, opened it up, and slid the scroll out?"

"It would appear so."

"Why not take the scroll case? It must be valuable too."

"Very valuable, in its own right, but practically worthless compared to the scroll. And removing the scroll case would trigger an alarm."

"I see. What type of alarm mechanism?"

"Pressure switch, which will also detect vibration, to a degree—If the scroll case were moved, the alarm would sound instantly."

"But the mechanism isn't sensitive enough to detect the loss of the scroll's weight, or the case opening?"

"Apparently not, it was calibrated for a heavy bronze item. Though they must have been exceptionally careful, to open it without setting off the vibration sensor."

I circled the exhibit, examining it thoughtfully.

"How heavy is the top?"

"It is solid brass. It took four men to lift it when it was installed."

"How is the display opened?"

"The display does not open, per se. It was assembled from base to top, and can only be accessed by disassembling it in reverse."

"So in short, you're saying that they somehow got all the way in here, popped this ridiculously heavy solid brass top off, very carefully removed the scroll without triggering the alarm, replaced the lid, and got out, all without being seen? Where are the cameras?"

I looked around and found a single camera, connected to the top of the guard booth and pointed down at Brevig's display.

"You only need one feed to cover this chamber," Spindlebrock declared. "I watched the video from the night of the crime, and found nothing amiss. I'll take you to watch it after lunch."

"Surely they altered the video."

"I don't think so. These cameras have a digital signature encoded in the feed. I called Lewis about it last night, he helped develop the technology."

I sighed and folded my arms.

"We're looking at an impossible crime. The burglar came into the building through an impossible entrance, somehow got to the inner vault without being seen, broke into this exhibit without triggering the alarm—"

"It gets worse. The scroll case is a sort of combination lock. There are twenty discs, each an icosagon with twenty sides, covered in runes—"

"Wait, you said Bronze Age, right? With a combination lock?" I interrupted.

"Late Bronze Age, yes. I confess that the lock mechanism is unique, an early example of a tumbler which doesn't quite fit into the Northern European landscape of the period, though it was in use elsewhere in the world by then. Keep in mind that magicians have long been more connected across societies, and more traveled than the—in any case, this is a question of the missing scroll, not the case."

"Right. So you're saying they figured out the combination, then? If that was a possibility, why didn't you secure the case more thoroughly?"

"No, there was no way they could manipulate the discs without setting off the vibration sensor. The runes must be carefully aligned before the case will open—and only Lucas Brevig knows the combination, since he set the tumblers.

Furthermore, the random order of the runes, which I have committed to memory, is undisturbed from when the display was first installed. Somehow, they got the scroll case open without the combination."

"Is it possible they disabled your sensors?"

"Not without that fact being in the security logs; they're network connected. I can monitor them from anywhere, actually. Taking them off the network would have triggered an alarm."

I laughed.

"So, what are we doing here? There's no mystery to solve. It's impossible."

"And yet, it happened."

"Well, I hope he had insurance."

Spindlebrock took his turn sighing.

"No amount of insurance could cover something this valuable. This vault was the insurance. I was the insurance."

Spindlebrock looked careworn.

"Look, Spindlebrock, you haven't slept. There's nothing you could have done, apparently. Whoever did this, knew exactly how to pull it off."

"And, without a trace. Not so much as a fingerprint."

We decided to break for lunch, but Spindlebrock's words, "without a trace" turned over and over in my head as we ate. The burglar, though certainly adept, was not a specter. They had left traces, such as showing up on the exterior video feed, and leaving bits of fabric in the crack where they scaled the wall. And yet, the inner vault seemed so entirely devoid of clues that further pursuit seemed meaningless.

As we finished eating I was about to suggest that Spindlebrock get some sleep, when a member of the hotel staff arrived at our table and handed the professor a letter. He opened and read it, then carefully folded it and placed it is in his pocket. I waited anxiously for several long moments before he spoke.

"Thomas, you said the case was impossible?"

"I did."

"How impossible?"

I shrugged. The question made no sense.

"I've just had word from Brevig. He's offering a substantial reward for the return of his scroll."

I wiped my mouth and set my napkin on my plate.

"Good. Maybe whoever stole it will take it as a ransom payment."

"I've had a thought. You've got debts, after so much schooling. Wouldn't it be nice to pay them all off? If we work together, we can split the reward."

"Sure, but that doesn't change the definition of the word impossible."

"Come now! If this burglary was carried out, it can be unraveled. Your craft, your trade is the formalization of the very idea!"

"I don't know, so far it seems like it will be a waste of time. Plus, I came here with Olivia, and we're supposedly poised to discover great things in the supernatural realm. She's not going to like the idea of turning this into a futile treasure hunt."

"And you'll be able to pursue those studies, rest assured. Besides, maybe she would want in on the reward as well?"

"Just how big is this reward?"

Spindlebrock removed the letter from his pocket and tossed it to me. The sum typed there was enough to comfortably secure all three of us for the rest of our natural lives. I opened my mouth several times to speak, but the words didn't come.

"Think of it Thomas, this kind of money would allow you the freedom to pursue your studies, hobbies—anything —for the rest of your days."

I did think. I'm not sure how long I looked at the figure on that letter. Ultimately, while large sums of money certainly have a voice, it was the thought that Spindlebrock really needed to fix this problem that tipped the scales for me. It may sound like self-aggrandizement to make the claim, but my friend's feelings were at the forefront of my mind. I didn't have a lot of hope, but I was determined to keep on going.

"I still don't believe there's much chance, and I still say Olivia won't go for it, but I can't ignore the possibilities this reward would open up. Let's keep working on it today, and we'll talk to Olivia about it when she gets back."

Spindlebrock was pleased. The rest of the afternoon was spent looking at video footage, and in visiting and revisiting different parts of the casino. Everywhere we went, we employed discovery charms of every description in pursuit of clues, but came up abjectly empty-handed. The video footage was just as disappointing. We scanned interior and exterior recordings from several days leading up to the burglary. We sifted through hours of recordings from various angles and in different areas. The footage from inside the inner vault was the most frustrating; we saw visitors, the guard, and the exhibits, but no sign of the moment when the scroll was taken. The feed was angled too low to capture the full scroll exhibit, cutting off before the glass reached the brass, and because of the distance of the camera you couldn't really tell whether the scroll case was opened or closed.

We watched and re-watched the moment when the guard realized that the scroll case was ajar, and the chaos that ensued. Something about it bothered me, but I couldn't tell what. By the end of the day, I was feeling even more hopeless about our prospects, and annoyed at the thought of bringing the idea of helping Spindlebrock up to Olivia.

It was late when she returned. Spindlebrock, exhausted from being up for so long, had gone to bed. I was sitting in the lobby enjoying some tea. She was so thrilled by her day's adventures, and I was so disheartened by mine, that I couldn't bring myself to mention Brevig's letter and the professor's proposal. Instead, I sat and listened to her interesting tale. As it is very much related to the rest of this book, I want you to have it. Rather than attempt to write it from my memory I've asked Olivia to write it out, and with very few edits (as I promised her), I share it with you now.

Chapter 6

Meeting Sanjay

My name is Olivia Zhang. I'm currently a post-grad student at the University of Magic, Toronto, studying applied physics and particle theory. Thomas asked me to write about my first trip to Sathyamangalam, India, because he felt I would do a better job relaying the details. Writing personal narratives makes me uncomfortable; he's the one writing books, but his project has brought enough unwanted attention that I'm glad to have a chance to share my story in my own way for once.

Though he did not give me his manuscript to review, I was assured that you would have already heard how we got to be in India, what brought us there, and what we were up to. To what he provided I will add that our trip took a lot of careful planning, as we had to fit it in to our school and work schedules, and we had to make the trip on very tight personal budgets. I will also add that the trip was a culmination of many years of work and research on my part, and that it had great personal meaning for me.

I'm aware of the fact that most people, even in the commonality, don't believe in ghosts. I accept their skepticism and invite discourse. What I cannot tolerate is indifference, prejudgment, and the sort of toxic condescension that I've encountered in many magicians over the years. If you can't stomach the experiences and discoveries of others when they don't agree with your preconceived notions, then I suggest you move along. I will not sugar-coat what I know.

My first trip to Sathyamangalam started out in frustration. I was in India with the help of professor Spindlebrock, who at the time I primarily knew as an academic leader. Thomas and I were going there to study metaphysical anomalies such as ghosts and/or spirits, when the whole business with the scroll came along. Spindlebrock wanted Thomas' help, and I was in the way. At least, that's the way I viewed it at first. He sent me off. For more than three hours I bumped around in a hot cab thinking about how they had simply gotten rid of me.

When I arrived at the home of Sanjay Mehan, I was not in a good mood. Somehow he seemed to understand, before he ever saw me. He had a young child there to help around the house—the boy struck me as British based on the accent, and he was pale with bright red hair—who invited me in to a quiet and cool sitting room, and seated me comfortably. A relaxing herb tea and a snack were waiting there for me, all ready to go. The child said that Sanjay would join me in about ten minutes, and I was left to cool off both literally and figuratively.

In the room there were two small bookshelves. I noticed that they were filled with many books I had already read, on the subject of ghosts, as well as many books I had never seen before. Some of these new books were in English, others were not. Some looked very old. I was curious, so I picked one up and started flipping through it—to my great surprise and delight, I found a plethora of handwritten notes. Believe it or not, these notes seemed to directly address particular ideas that I had struggled with, and so as I sat there, I started to have a strong desire to speak with this Sanjay fellow. It was just as that desire turned into an anxiousness for him to arrive, that he came into the room.

Sanjay was old and frail. I got up when he came in, and felt like I should help him walk, but he knowingly motioned for me to sit back down. He poured me another cup of tea, and one for himself, and sat down next to me.

Immediately, he delved into the very subject I had been reading about in his notes. In simple terms, it was the subject of the manipulation of matter, and the nature of spirits and spiritual matter—I guess what I mean is, sort of the science behind the ghost phenomenon, and what it means in the physical world. Parts of it are sometimes lumped in with a larger magical discipline called elemental magic. Thomas said that many of his readers are non-magical, so I'll just explain real quick that in the magical commonality elemental magic is usually referring to things related to the physical elements, like telekinesis. But it's also about elements that you can't perhaps directly see, and that's what I was interested in.

Sanjay shared stories and asked questions, and gave me valuable insights on these topics. It felt so natural, so unforced, like I was talking to an old friend about a subject that we had studied together for years.

Then, just as suddenly as he had started talking, he stopped, and said this:

"There is a block inside you, a wall. We must address it before we can go any further."

He caught me off guard, but he was so soft-spoken and so kind that I had no defense. I didn't know what he was going to get at, but at that point I didn't care. I felt his respect for me, and I really believed he could help me, so I accepted what he had to say.

Of course, he would have to bring up Spindlebrock. I say that jokingly now, but at the time it was a hard subject. I had some serious resentments toward the professor. Spindlebrock and I have talked about it quite a bit since then, and so I'm OK with sharing all of this with you now, knowing that he understands, and I understand. At this point in my narrative, though, I didn't really understand the professor, and Sanjay seemed to know it.

Sanjay helped me identify my resentments. He told me they were like gnarled logs floating down a flooded river;

they would bang around and cause damage, and eventually all get jammed together and cause a block. He told me of a river that he knew as a child, that would flood every monsoon season, and that would fill with all kinds of dangerous debris.

To be honest, I think the only reason I let him talk me through those emotional subjects was—and I'm a little ashamed to admit this—it was because I wanted so badly to know what he knew. I figured that he wouldn't work with me unless I came on his terms. I misunderstood him, of course, but that's what I thought at the time, and it got me started. He was so kind though, and in a very short time he simply helped me realize that I was carrying weight that I didn't need to carry, and that it was slowing me down.

We talked about my hangups for an hour or two. I let it flow, and it felt liberating. And then something amazing happened. He thanked me, then closed his eyes and breathed in very deeply. With a faint smile on his face, he started to exhale, and while he did, he began to hum. At least, I thought he was humming. There was definitely a humming sound. The room began to get brighter, I thought, but then I noticed that it was only getting brighter directly around him. I was transfixed. He got brighter and brighter, and I couldn't pull my eyes away. Then, he became transparent, and just at that moment he opened his eyes, but they weren't the tired old eyes that I had seen just moments earlier, they were young and full of energy. Then, maybe from the excitement or for some other reason, I fainted.

When I came to, Sanjay was gone. I thought that perhaps I had fallen asleep and dreamed the whole thing up, but then I noticed the two cups of tea sitting on the small table. Just as I arose to go and search for him, the young boy came in and announced that Sanjay was in the garden. He asked me to follow him, which I did eagerly. We found Sanjay meditating, but as I approached he opened his eyes (they were the tired eyes of old age, once again) and addressed me.

"Spindlebrock is one of my oldest friends."

He went on to explain in very vague terms, that he and Spindlebrock had done a great deal of research on ghosts and elemental magic together, and that many of the answers that he now possessed, he had arrived at with the professor by his side. Apparently, he was Professor Spindlebrock's guru in a sense, and he viewed the professor as a pupil. I was stunned. I asked him what happened in the sitting room, and he only answered, "Before the end of the day, I will tell you what you have seen."

What happened next was rather extraneous, I thought at the time, but it was part of the experience and training that I was to receive that day; and it was in reality highly educational. Sanjay had a cab take us to a local shop, where they were advertising a so-called "haunted exhibition." All the locals knew him. He asked them to explain to me what kinds of tours were available, what I might see, costs, and every other mundane detail. They obliged readily. Their descriptions of what I knew to be fabricated experiences were irritating to me, but Sanjay seemed to understand when I had had enough. As we walked out to the car, he made some comments that stuck with me.

"Olivia, I think Spindlebrock sent you to me so that you might become my pupil. You want to know about ghosts and spirits and manifestations; this is an acceptable place to start. The people who come to these businesses to go on a haunted exhibition, they also have curiosity. Can you place yourself next to those people? Can you say that you are one with the good people who offer exhibitions of this kind? You think that you understand all these people, but you need to be more at peace with them, because they are like you, except that you know and understand more of some things, and they of others. In the same way, you are like me. When you judge these people, what happens to you? Would it be better if you didn't judge them, but saw them as versions of yourself in some way?"

I thought hard about what he said. After we left, Sanjay took us to a mountainside, near a jungle, where some sort of floating lights were said have been spotted, according to the people we had just left. It was apparently a very well known spot, and one that was viewed as authentic; even the cab driver seemed nervous. After we got out, we walked a short way into the dense woods, when we started hearing distant screams. Sanjay shouted out a few words in some Tamil dialect, and several men came forward from the underbrush with warm greetings. After a short conversation, the men seemed to bid him goodbye, and we started into the forest down a very narrow path. The screams stopped; I assumed that the men were there to frighten tourists, and that Sanjay informed them that we were not their target audience.

We must have walked about an hour in silence, sometimes on one of the many paths, sometimes straight through underbrush to connect to other more hidden paths. I don't know how he kept track, as it felt like we were walking in circles. The jungle woods were serene, but the thought of what might be lurking in there eventually became loud in my mind. Sanjay sensed this, I think, and reassured me that nothing would happen. We saw no animal or person the entire walk.

Eventually we came to a dry riverbed.

"Here," he said, "is one place where those who are willing to work may come."

"Willing to work on what?"

"All learning is work. You wish to discover things about ghosts and the elements and matter—you called it spirit matter, but it is all the same though on different planes of existence. A wish to know these things is not enough to learn them. You must work, and this is one place where you may do that kind of work. I will show you. I will teach you."

From his pocket, Sanjay removed a smooth white stone. He held it out, but not for me to take. I looked at it for a moment, before he pulled it away. Smiling, he reached down into the riverbed, and pulled out a stone. It was smooth, but dark gray.

"You can see, these are two different stones. You can perhaps also see that one is much more pure than the other. I want you to consider the reasons for this as you learn."

He handed the gray stone to me, and we began to walk again, this time down the riverbed. We eventually stopped, and both sat on a log.

"Look there."

I looked where Sanjay pointed, and saw a tangle of logs and vines. I asked what it was, and was told to go and see for myself. I did, and found that it was a sort of raft or canoe. Sanjay informed me that it was called a kattumaram, and asked me to examine it more closely. It was covered with ancient carved writing that I could make nothing of.

"Sit on the kattumaram, please. There, in the middle. Take the gray stone and set it in front of you, it will help you focus. It is a tangible object with an intangible quality that you do not yet know. You will learn that there are many planes, many spheres of existence, and that you may move through them in certain ways, until you reach the ultimate plane in a future life. In these planes, objects also exist. But you cannot learn any of this by being told, any more than you can learn to ride a bike simply by hearing about it. You must do, in order to truly learn."

He came close as I sat on the old boat. Placing his hands on the wood, he explained that he would read some of the ancient words, and that I was not to get off the raft no matter what happened. He was really forceful on the point, warning of all kinds of dire but nondescript consequences. As he read, I was to repeat a spell which he taught me there on the spot. It was in an ancient language, but the sounds were simple enough to memorize. He explained the meaning as well; the words were about connection and separation, oneness and distinctness. It seemed to be almost prayer-like in quality, a supplication to reach for something higher. I didn't fully understand it, but I learned it.

As he started to read, I began the incantation. Then, my world came apart at the seams.

First, the dry riverbed started to fill rapidly with water. I thought I felt it move the kattumaram, and soon I felt the sensation of bobbing, then drifting. I turned to Sanjay and saw that he was glowing and becoming translucent. Panic struck my heart, but I remembered his dire warnings and continued my own incantation. Before long, Sanjay had disappeared, and I was careening down a flooding jungle river. I was terrified, but I clung to the raft and didn't budge.

While this was happening, I continued to hear the words that Sanjay was reading. I couldn't see him, but his voice was louder than the raging waters, and louder than my own voice, which felt like it was being drowned out. I was about to give up and scream for help, but at that very moment, Sanjay stopped reading and said, "Focus on the rock as you move to another plane."

Somehow I knew what he meant. I focused all of my thought on the meaning of the words I was speaking, the spell he had taught me and its translation. I thought of the rock, and how the physical manifestation of it was not all the reality that there was. Then, without meaning to, I thought of Spindlebrock, and the magical tourism people, and the idea of being at peace with them all. As I did so, the rock in front of me started to glow, then it became translucent. All of a sudden, the glowing rock started to rise —leaving the gray rock sitting where it was. There were now two stones. The one in the air before me was glowing white.

"Take the new stone."

It was his voice again, breaking through all that was going on. I seemed to hear it overlaying over his reading voice, over the rushing water, over my own voice. As I reached forward to take the stone, I saw that my own hand was glowing and translucent, and I wondered if I was in my own body. As my hand closed around it, everything suddenly stopped.

I was back in the quiet jungle. My head was still reeling, but I was back, and everything was back to normal. Clutching the stone in my hand, I looked around me. I looked down, and saw the gray stone still sitting on the boat. Confused, I opened my palm and saw a lighter stone that matched it in every way but in color.

"That did not take nearly as long as I thought it might! You are indeed very gifted, Olivia, just as the professor said!"

He helped me off the kattumaram. Though I hadn't actually gone anywhere, I still felt the need to catch my breath and steady myself, as I reconnected my feet with the Earth.

"I promised you that I would explain what you saw earlier, while we were sitting in my house and you forgave Professor Spindlebrock in your heart. What you witnessed in me was elevation to a very slightly higher plane. I helped you overcome your block, and in doing so I had an opportunity to be lifted myself—such opportunities come throughout our lives if we let them. The elements in me shifted because of your thoughts and my thoughts, and in that moment I felt what to do in my heart and mind—there is much magic that can be done without words, if you have enough knowledge and experience. You did not see me take the stone, which I use to focus, because you were overwhelmed and unfocused. But I did take the new iteration of my own stone at that time.

"Each time I do this, the stone becomes more and more pure, as it is from a different and higher plane. It is not me that purifies it, but I must reach out and take it, and keep it, and keep working on it. The stone is a symbol, but it is also a tangible proof, a connection, and an evidence of your movements. It reminds you, and encourages you, and guides you. Keep your stone with you at all times, and remember the words that I have taught you. Remember to focus, and to help others. You may perhaps never come back to this particular place of training, but you have now learned the way and can draw on it always. Like riding a bicycle, you know what it means now, and can practice.

"With your natural gifts and talents, you will find opportunities to move through many planes in your life, to experience them in different ways. Always seek higher planes. Those who have passed on, have passed into other planes—Those beings who you have seen—"

He paused and looked at me a long time before continuing.

"They wanted to be seen."

He also gave me warnings and encouragement and instruction that I won't share here. The point is, my seeking after ghosts and spirits—and the helpful actions of Professor Spindlebrock in sending me to Sanjay—led me toward a different understanding and goal, one that I still seek after today. I was no longer a ghost hunter, as some might call it. I was a pupil, a student of a discipline that I hadn't really understood at all until that day, though I had certainly heard and seen hints of it scattered about my studies.

Leaving the jungle was a blur to me—it almost felt as if we were just suddenly back on the very end of our path, saying goodbye to the tourist screamers. Before I left his house that evening, I thanked him and hugged him and promised to return as his pupil, a promise that I have kept as often as I could so far.

And that's the short version of what happened to me that day. Take it for what you will, but it did happen, whether you believe it or not.

Chapter 7

A Ghastly Tour

The morning after Olivia's return, the Professor woke me early. He was fully dressed, and wore a look of concern on his brow.

"They've called a tribunal."

"What?" I was still only half awake.

"A tribunal, called by Lowen. He's extremely concerned about the value of the scroll, what its loss might mean to me personally, and how this might appear for his business. We discussed options, and I suggested he call a local tribunal."

I sat up in bed.

"It was your idea? What about our investigation?"

"Well, there's no reason it has to entirely stop. The tribunal will be largely a matter of show, to demonstrate to all his customers that Lowen is taking matters very seriously. You'll be able to continue the investigation on your own, though you will need to work more on the sidelines, staying out of the way as we make our inquiries."

"What do you mean 'we'? You said it was a local tribunal, I thought local tribunals had to be comprised of people who lived here—and aren't you too closely connected to the case to be chosen?"

"It's a long sort of story, ultimately, but I lived here years ago, and that was apparently enough for the selection process. I have many close friends here. Some of the tribunal members argued that they consider me local, and given the gravity of the situation, none wanted to pass up my experience, even though I am connected to Brevig and the case."

This may sound unusual to those who know about the politics surrounding local tribunal investigations, which are almost universally comprised of respected magicians residing in the area where the tribunal is called; but I couldn't really find fault with the logic of the arrangement.

"Lowen wasn't too pleased about me being on the tribunal: I think he believed I would continue my investigation with you, uninterrupted. Plus, if the tribunal were to find a guilty party, my connection with Brevig would mean that I wouldn't be allowed to take part in leveling charges—but none of that matters much. With your time more open, you and Olivia will get your opportunity to pursue that ghost you came here for. That should keep you and me out of hot water, if you know what I mean."

I knew he meant with Olivia, but I didn't say anything. He continued.

"And when you're not working on that project, Lowen has instructed his staff to help you however they can with the scroll investigation. You'll have plenty of time to do both —I'm late already, the tribunal will be waiting for me, I should be going."

"How long will the tribunal take? Will I see you at all?"

"It'll probably take a few days at the most, and I'll be in late. We may not see one another, even in the evenings. Wish me luck!"

I had concerns that were unresolved, but with my best wishes and a handshake, he was gone.

At breakfast, Olivia tried to act indifferent to the news of his involvement, but she was crestfallen to hear that Spindlebrock would be difficult to get in touch with for a while, as she sincerely wished to thank him for arranging the meeting with Sanjay.

"I mean," she said between bites of toast and sips of tea, "considering what I learned yesterday, I'm starting to reconsider my whole notion of what these manifestations actually are. I was total worn out last night, but I still couldn't help going over the day in my head."

"It sounds like it was amazing."

"It was! Somehow I never really connected some of these lines, between spirits and ghosts, planes of existence—

everything! I hardly know where to start, my mind is racing so fast."

I gulped my orange juice.

"Well, we're here, and we've got time now. What if we just start where we were going to start in the first place? We were going to look into this story with Daksh—the case that Spindlebrock recommended."

"Huh? Sure, that's as good an idea as any at this point."

She was distracted, mindlessly pushing a small pile of fruit from one side of her plate to the other. Something had changed in her.

"I thought you were quite interested in the sighting? When the Professor shared it originally, you were full of questions, enthusiastic even."

"I know, it's just—I guess it's just that my whole mind has been shifted somehow, like the goals that I had aren't as important as I thought they were. Does that make sense? But maybe you're right—maybe we need to look into it. It'll give us something to do, anyway. And it's what we came here for, who knows what we may learn."

"Right," I said, pulling out my notebook. "So, where do we start?"

"I guess here, at the casino. Spindlebrock said that he saw him here, right?"

"He did. I wish he would have told us where."

"What do you mean?"

"I mean, this hotel is big, and parts of it are ancient—he could have seen the ghost anywhere. In your studies on the subject, would you say that knowing the location of a sighting might increase your chances of repeating the sighting?"

Olivia pushed her plate aside and began to focus.

"Sure, that's usually the case. Some people describe ghost sightings as a loop of sorts, where the spirit is repeating the same action or event over and over again."

"OK, that's one lead we can count on then. When we get a chance, we'll ask Spindlebrock where he saw Daksh."

"Who knows when that will be."

"That's true. Any ideas on where we could start in the meantime?"

"We could ask around, see if they have any records about the history of this place—but I'm guessing those records would be artifacts, stored or locked up. How 'bout you, any ideas?"

I had one, but it didn't seem like one that Olivia would like. She sensed my uneasiness.

"Oh, come on. We've come half-way around the world to be here, just spit it out."

"I don't know, I was thinking that we might find something—however unlikely—on the guided tour."

"The tour? You mean the haunted tour? Seriously?"

"Why not? We've got time, and it could put us in touch with some people who might know something."

She scoffed, shaking her head, then suddenly sat bolt upright.

"You know, you might have something there. Remember when I told you about how Sanjay took me into the jungle? We stopped by a sort of tour agency first, for guided ghost tours."

"Yes, I remember, you said that you thought they were a bunch of frauds, or something like that."

"They were, but at the same time, they were connected. They knew Sanjay, and he knew them. He knew them well, I'd say—they seemed to be friends. And, I think they understood that even though they were selling a fake experience, there was something real in it. Besides, he asked me to view them differently."

She tapped on the table, pondering.

"Maybe the tour guides here are connected to someone who knows something—something real—about Daksh. We could at least ask around. Talking to them couldn't hurt."

We both agreed that interviewing the staff who handled the guided tours would be a good place to start. The front desk directed us to the courtyards at the rear of the casino complex, beyond the swimming pools and their associated bars and lounge areas. It was a beautiful, if hot day. The pools were busy, but the courtyards beyond, filled with gardens and canopy-shaded walking paths, were not nearly as frequented as they might have been. As we wound through them, we encountered only a handful of guests.

Signs led us through the courtyard paths, to a small structure near the edge of the jungle forest. I would have called it a shack, but it was made primarily of stacked stones, and the word somehow didn't quite fit. The inside was clean, though the floor was of dirt. A single worker sat behind a plain wood desk.

"Good afternoon," he said in thickly accented English, bowing his head slightly. "Welcome to the Quarters. Are you here to register for the tour this evening?"

"Not exactly," I responded. "We just have a few questions."

"I see. Perhaps you would want to arrange a private tour?"

"Uh, no. We're looking for information, about a—well, about Daksh Parikh."

The worker looked at us questioningly.

"Parikh, huh? I don't know him, does he work at the casino, or is he a guest?"

Olivia chimed in.

"He's a ghost. He was named Daksh Parikh. We've heard that he has been sighted here, at the Cascabela."

The worker smiled.

"Ah, yes, Parikh! Yes, now you are talking about something I can tell you about."

The man started in on a story, memorized and scripted, of a series of ghosts that had haunted the hills where the Cascabela was built, time out of mind. Here and there he sprinkled in the name Parikh, where he thought it might be impressive or important. When he was through, he leaned forward over the desk and spoke in a whisper.

"To see Parikh, you should come back in just a few hours, when the sun is over the very top of the mountain and on its way almost down to the horizon. I will have a private guide to take you then, to the place where he is seen —and, because you are in the know, you know, I will give you a special rate."

We thanked him, and headed back toward the courtyards.

"Well, that was a waste of time. He clearly knew nothing," Olivia observed.

"That's true, and even if he did know something, I'm not sure we would have been able to get a straight answer out of him. He was pretty well set on selling us a tour."

"Exactly. A great employee, but not a great source of info. Do you think he's the only one working the tour?"

"Well," I ventured, "from what we can surmise of these kinds of tourist attractions, there would likely be a crew out in the forest ready to jump-scare, or control whatever they've got rigged up. But good luck getting him to admit that."

Olivia was quiet as we returned to the casino. As we were about to enter, she turned back and gazed at the wooded mountain.

"I want to go back. We'll try the tour, just to say that we exhausted the option—does that sound good?"

"I guess it couldn't hurt. But we have a few hours to burn before the tour starts. Should we try to find more info, maybe ask the staff inside?"

She was distracted, and still staring at the woods.

"No—I'm sorry, I'm a little lost. Maybe it's the time change. Honestly, I'd like to clear my mind of ghosts and spirits and things for a bit. What if you show me the vault while we wait?"

I agreed and we started on our way, when I suddenly recalled that I hadn't updated her Brevig's letter or

Spindlebrock's idea about splitting the reward mentioned therein. As we walked I explained the core facts I had learned concerning the lost scroll and the intruder from the woods, before sharing what the letter contained.

"Wow," she said at length. "And he sent this to Spindlebrock? Doesn't it seem a little like a slap in the face—like saying that he really doesn't believe that the professor can get it back?"

"I don't know, I guess I didn't see it that way. It just seemed like desperation to me, like he was trying to tell him that he could have anything he needed to get the job done—but I don't know Brevig, or anything about their relationship."

"Yeah, me neither. Well, I certainly wouldn't complain about splitting a reward, even though I'm not sure how exactly I would fit in this whole thing. Is this it?"

We were at the entrance to the vaults. I explained the design as we walked through the vaults and toward the center. Once there, I showed her the exhibit.

"How does the display open?"

"It was assembled from base to top. The only way in is to remove the top, then remove the glass tube, and so forth."

"The top looks really heavy."

"Spindlebrock said it took four men to put it in place. It's solid brass."

"That seems a bit excessive—and the scroll was inside the fancy holder, I'm guessing."

"Yep."

"What are the runes for?"

"They're part of a combination lock system."

"So the burglar knew the combination?"

"No, they got it open some other way, it seems."

"Not a very good lock, if you can just pop it open without the combination. Are there any signs of it being forced open?"

"Couldn't have been forced, the whole thing sits on a system that would have been triggered if it was lifted or jarred."

"Fingerprints?"

"None. No trace that anything was moved or touched, actually."

"Well, I suppose a magician did it, otherwise we'd have more physical evidence."

I laughed, quite without thinking. Olivia seemed offended.

"What?"

"Well, I mean, I think we already knew this was the work of a magician."

"Oh, really? And so you didn't even bother to rule out a more conventional job, then?"

I started to mutter a reply, but she continued.

"Come on! You're supposed to be a forensic scientist, aren't you! Rule things out, and see what's left!"

I took a deep breath and tried to look at the situation objectively. I saw nothing new.

"You'll see, when you get a chance to watch the video, that there was no apparent issue with the display. Guards are constantly on duty, surveillance is in place, and there was no indication of tampering, especially not of the conventional type."

"Did you interview him? The guard, I mean."

"It was her, I believe, but the video isn't perfectly clear. I haven't interviewed the guard myself, not yet at least."

"Why not?"

"Our investigation was interrupted, with the tribunal being called. Lowen spoke with the guards already, Spindlebrock said he interviewed them all. We certainly would have too—we still will. I'm sure the tribunal will as well, if they haven't already."

"Well, it really does look rather bleak. I'm guessing you're not investing your heart and soul into the thought of that reward."

"I'm definitely not—I'm doing this for Spindlebrock."

"Good call. I guess I'll help for the same reason, if I can be of any help. I know that's what Sanjay would want—and come to think of it, that's what I want too."

With no new clues, and with the tour starting soon, we made our way through the building toward the rear exit and into the pool area. We paused to watch the swimmers as we traversed the courtyard, when without warning a voice accosted us from one of the nearby bars.

"Hey, hello! You there! You are headed for the haunted tours, yes?"

Olivia and I looked at one another, then at the man behind the bar. His face was in the shadows.

"Come! Come close!"

We stepped closer, and saw that it was the same worker who had sold us on the tour earlier.

"It's me! I saw you walking there, and said that maybe you were coming back after all. You looked like a brave couple, I thought surely you would be back, right?"

Olivia inched away from me at the word "couple".

"Yes," I responded to the worker. "We're just headed that way now."

"Oh, don't worry!" he replied, though I certainly hadn't expressed any concern. "I told them to give you the special rate, yes, just like I said I would, you see!"

He looked around, motioning for us to come closer, which we did.

"And just so you know this isn't something I always do, alright? I'm going to give you some free drinks too, to help you on the way!"

He turned toward a row of bottles behind him, and started running his fingers across them back and forth, as if making a careful selection.

"I don't drink," I blurted out. Olivia looked between us, and added a, "No, thank you."

The worker whirled around.

"No, no! No worries friends! I make you the virgin drink style, no alcohol! It's very good, you'll see!"

As he was insistent, and as we still had a little time before the tour, we took a seat and waited as he prepared our drinks. The drinks were white like coconut milk, with a slightly fruity odor that I couldn't place. We sat and enjoyed them to the chatter of the worker, which was a pleasant distraction.

Before we knew it, we had made our way to the forest, paid the supposedly-reduced fee, and started on the haunted tour. Our guide was another salesman type, who spoke in hushed tones as we entered the wooded trail. The sun was setting rapidly, and the woods were dull and gloomy.

Our first stop on the tour was a sort of stone shrine, in the shape of a human-like creature, entwined with strangling vines. Two dark holes, like eyes, were in the stomach, which stood at about eye-level.

"This is a bhoota, a churel of a woman who lived in these woods long ago. It is said that to look in the stomach you see a bhoota of her son, who she never knew in life, but who cannot escape now to Swarga."

Our guide moved closer.

"Come, and look. You will see. The bhoota is small and white, and his feet are on backwards."

This last line, "small and white, with feet on backwards", was repeated by the guide over and over, as he ushered us up to the two holes in the shrine's belly. I leaned forward and peered into the darkness. At first I saw nothing, but as I stared a faint white glimmer started to grow. It grew until it became strong, and took form. I felt paralyzed and my stomach churned as I saw the form of a child appear. As the shape grew more distinct, I saw that its feet were indeed on backwards.

I started, stumbling away from the shrine with a shriek. Olivia smiled, and stepped up to take her turn. Moments later, she screamed.

I'm not sure how we arrived at the next stop, as I don't recall walking there, I only remember shaking. The next stop was what looked like the bank of a dry river bank. Stone steps lay crumbling before a small beach of white sand.

"This is the Mountain Ghat, the kaadu. It is no longer used, of course, for a thousand years. But the white sand stays here undisturbed. It contains a part of the ashes from the shmashana that used to be here. It is said that to step on the first step requires the bravery of Tekhumiavi, the Tiger-Man, and to step down to the sand is insanity. What will you see if you try it? Step up, step up and see the white cloth floating where the shmashana stood. Come and see the white cloth..."

Without thinking, I found myself wandering to the first step, as the guide repeated the words, "come and see the white cloth". Olivia was standing by my side, fixated as I was on the white sand. Much as with our first stop, a glimmer of white transformed into the form of a white cloth. Just as before, the shape came clearer and clearer, until it appeared to be a wrapped body floating before us.

The guide shouted something in his native language, we stumbled backward on the steps and fell sitting on the path, and the apparition was gone.

Getting up felt sluggish, and I noted that walking felt like movement in my upper-body but not in my legs. We arrived at our final destination, which was a small hut at a fork in the road.

"Now, my friends, I cannot go further. In this building here, I must wait in safety until the effects of the forest are gone. What you have seen, I have not seen, and I cannot know. You must choose now—"

Here he motioned toward the path on our left.

"Go this way deeper into the forest, and you may see more. Or—"

Now, he motioned to the path on our right.

"This path will lead you quickly back to the light and civilization. Both paths will take you safely back to the Cascabela. You must choose."

And with that, he stepped back into the darkness of the hut, leaving us alone.

My instinct was to rush headlong on the short path back to the casino, and I started to head that way without even consulting my companion. But as soon as my feet started moving, Olivia stopped me, pulling my arm until my ear was at the level of her mouth.

"If we don't do this now, we won't ever have the guts to come back," she whispered.

My feet were starting to tingle, like they do when they've been out in the cold for too long, and the beginning of a headache was throbbing at the base of my neck. I looked at the two paths, and knew she was right. We started off on the path to our left.

As we walked, my head started to clear, but I didn't know what to say. Olivia spoke first.

"That was unexpected."

"What did you see?" I asked, anxiously hoping that my experience wasn't singular.

She thought silently as we walked, before finally answering.

"I saw just what he told me to see. First, a child—a little girl in a white dress, floating, with her feet backwards."

"A girl? I saw a little boy!"

"Then," she continued, "I just saw a white cloth floating in the air. I didn't know what to make of it."

I pondered.

"Do you know what a shmashana is?" I queried.

"No."

"It's a place where cremations are performed," I explained. "I saw a white cloth wrapped around a body."

88

"So, we both saw what our minds produced. And it seemed to be based on what our so-called guide prompted. But that doesn't explain—"

She paused, thrusting her hand out in front of me, her palm on my chest as if to stop me in my tracks. I obeyed, my senses on full alert.

"Do you see this?"

I looked around the dim woods. The path was presently interrupted by a wide, shallow ravine covered by a flat concrete bridge.

"What is it? All I see is an old river."

"I've been here before. Or, somewhere like it..."

Without another word, Olivia walked off the path and started making her way down into the ravine. Still rattled, I was anxious to remain on the path, but I could see the casino and the edge of the woods a short way down the old riverbed, and so I followed in silence.

After we reached the center of the ravine and traveled a few steps, we both heard a voice.

"Will you walk with me?"

Turning, I saw a young man. He looked more or less normal at first, with the exception of his clothing, which looked out of time. He was Indian, but his clothes were more or less European, and he spoke with a British accent.

Neither Olivia nor I answered, but we followed as he walked on toward the casino.

"It's been such a long time since I've walked with anyone. Very few people take my path, and even fewer walk in my riverbed. I get so lonely."

As we walked, I began to realize that the young man wasn't actually touching the ground. His clothes, which appeared normal at first, were taking on a translucent white quality. I began to shake.

Olivia realized what was happening before I did. Without looking at the boy, she spoke.

"We've been hoping to see you. Is your name Daksh?"

The young man laughed.

"Yes!" Then in more serious tones, "How did you know?"

"We've come from far away just to see you."

Here she paused, and removed a light gray stone from her pocket. Daksh's eyes darted from the stone to Olivia, and then to the casino. A faint smile passed over his face.

"Is it time to try again?" he whispered.

Without another word, he vanished.

Chapter 8

A River Runs Through It

It was extremely late when Spindlebrock finally crept into the room. He was trying to make as little noise as possible so as not to wake me, but I was entirely unable to sleep owing to a massive headache that had set in after Olivia and I stumbled out of the woods. We followed the ravine, which turned into a drainage ditch leading right up to the back of the casino. We were both so fatigued from our experience that we made our way to our rooms without a word, and crashed in our beds.

When Spindlebrock entered, I spoke.

"Welcome back. How was the tribunal?"

The professor was shocked, I think, to find me so awake.

"The tribunal was profoundly ineffective—I think that tomorrow I'll have time to meet with you and Olivia for breakfast, to discuss it. But what are you doing up? Is everything alright?"

I rubbed my forehead and sat up in bed. I was still wearing my clothes from the day before. The clock read 1:51AM.

"Fine, yes. Everything is fine. We just had a rough time with the tour. It gave me a massive headache."

After a few moments, Spindlebrock seemed to understand that I meant the hotel's haunted tour. Comprehension flashed across his face. He sat next to me and grabbed my chin, examining my face and head as he turned it from side to side.

"Your pupils are excessively dilated. Did you eat or drink anything before the tour?"

"No, we just—well, yes, I guess. The bar at the pool gave us some free drinks before we went."

His eyebrows raised.

"Drinks? I thought you didn't—"

"Non-alcoholic, some kind of virgin coconut-milk drink I think, but it didn't really taste like coconut..."

I stammered as he fumbled in his bag. He pulled out several vials and sat down in the chair next to the bed.

"Did you both have the drinks? What did you each see on the tour?"

I answered his first question in the affirmative, then started to give a synopsis of the haunted tour. He stopped me mid-sentence.

"Do you trust me?"

In his outstretched hand he held three vials. I knew what he meant to do, and I normally would have gone along with it, but between the headache and jet lag and everything else, I lost my temper.

"Get those things out of my face," I grumbled. "Do I trust you? Do you still have to ask that, every time? I've taken every potion you've ever given me—of course I trust you. But my memory is just fine, and if you'll listen, I'll tell you exactly what happened."

A twinge of regret attempted to admonish me as he dejectedly put away the vials, but before I could say anything more, he spoke.

"I've never really thought about how much I ask that question. Honestly, I know that I do have trust issues in general, but you are right—you've always trusted me and I ought to express my trust in you more than I do."

Noticing that I was looking chagrined, he continued hastily and in a more gentle tone.

"Honestly, no hard feelings my friend! Now, continue where you left off, before I interrupted."

After a few more reassuring nods, I continued with my recounting of our haunted tour excursion. He listened intently, especially as I shared the details of our brief meeting with Daksh. When I was finished, he spoke again.

"I'd bet money that the barkeeper is in league with the tour guides. He likely drugged you both with a potion of some kind, Praesent Suggerum or the like—nothing nefarious, but not the most upstanding of business practices."

"It's my fault," he continued after a pause. "I should have warned you. Mixed drinks at a magical casino are risky; the ethics in a place like this are loose to begin with, but when it comes to what you drink they're even worse. In a normal casino, they manipulate their patrons with alcohol, as I'm sure you're aware. Here, they do it with mostly harmless suggestive potions. The results are related, but the magician's way is more deliberate, and more effective."

"Then why would anyone drink anything here?"

"Why would anyone drink alcohol at a non-magical casino? You don't think they understand what's going on there? Some people want to be misled, fogged, drugged—they think it makes their experience more enjoyable."

I tried to roll his point over in my aching mind, but at the time I couldn't quite grasp it. It makes perfect sense as I ponder on it now.

"So with the mixed drinks that were likely laced with potions, you were both quite susceptible to suggestion and experienced the tour as it was meant to be experienced, speaking from a marketing perspective. But at the end, when the tour was concluded and the potions were wearing off, you had an actual experience with Daksh, it seems, just as you had hoped. My only advice going forward would be to stick to water, juice, or other simple drinks."

"What good would that do? Many potions are odorless and tasteless," I scoffed.

"It's an unspoken code. Even in a place engineered to rob you there is a form of twisted honor. If you ask for water, juice, or something straight up, and they give you something else—they could be in for real trouble, and they know that. Remember, for them it's just business."

He pondered silently for several moments before continuing.

"You said that Olivia recognized the river in the woods?"

I confirmed his statement.

"And she had a stone?" he inquired, eyebrows raised high. I recalled that he hadn't heard about Olivia's visit with Sanjay.

"Yes, she got it from Sanjay, on her trip. Actually, she said that she visited a dry riverbed, in the jungle, I think it was. Maybe that's what she was talking about? You really have to hear her story."

He leaned back in his chair.

"Amazing. Yes, I think I really do need to hear that story. But that will have to wait until morning. You need some sleep, and I could do with some as well."

With a slight grin, he rummaged in his bag and pulled out yet another vial.

"I won't ask you to trust me blindly," he smiled. "This is to help with that headache, and the effects of the potion you took earlier."

I gladly took his potion, and drifted off to sleep.

It was closer to lunch by the time we all met up the next day. Our appetites were minimal, so we made our way outside with some plates of paratha bread. After some chatter, Spindlebrock asked Olivia if she would walk with him for a bit; I guessed then, and was proven correct later, that he wanted to hear all about her visit to Sanjay.

As they walked, I sat in the sun and applied my refreshed mind to the two problems that it was now facing: the scroll, and Daksh. In the matter of the scroll, I determined that I must secure an interview with Lowen and Spindlebrock, and the guard that was on duty in the inner chamber when the scroll was taken. There must be things only that guard knew, perspectives only they could give. Ultimately I concluded that I simply couldn't rely on notes from previous interviews; I needed to speak with them myself.

In the matter of Daksh, my mind took hold of a faint and featureless notion I somehow couldn't shake. I finished my paratha, followed by a glass of water (that I drank with some needless trepidation, given our experience the day before), and started back toward the haunted woods. Bypassing the guides entirely, I made my way to the concrete bridge over the ravine, near the spot where Daksh had appeared. He was, of course, nowhere to be seen.

In the noonday sun the scene was quite ordinary for that part of India—enchanting in its way, but not remarkable. In the interest of being thorough, I used a few spells to reveal any potential human movement through the underbrush, or other signs of human presence in the area surrounding the riverbed. Finding nothing, I scrambled into the ravine we had visited, and started to follow it toward the casino.

The fact that the concrete bridge was there meant that the ravine wasn't always dry—it must be used to direct the flow of rain water at times. There was a notion that I couldn't shake, that the flow of that seasonal river in relation to the casino was important—and so I followed it to see exactly where it led.

Just as the position at the bridge suggested, the original river went directly toward the casino. I recalled vaguely that we had stumbled through that way the night before, on our way back to our rooms. As I approached the courtyard and pools, a man-made concrete diversion took the ravine artificially around the north side of the complex. I walked through it, around the building, beyond the edge of the parking lot, and to the jungle-forest on the west entrance side of the property. There, after the parking lot, the concrete wash directed any potential seasonal water flow back toward the original riverbed.

My suspicion was confirmed: the river had once flowed directly through the current location of the Black Cascabela.

For a time I just stood in the wash, thinking and staring at the casino from afar. Why did they go to the trouble of diverting it, rather than just building the casino a few hundred yards away on higher ground? Or, given the age of the older parts of the building—not a casino originally, I corrected myself—did the wash perhaps form after they built the structure?

My pondering was interrupted by a group of security guards who were waving me down from the front entrance. As I approached, I realized from their behavior that they had been sent expressly to find me, and with some amount of concern.

"This jungle isn't a tenth as safe as it looks," Spindlebrock chided after the security guards escorted me back to him and Olivia. "You shouldn't wander off alone!"

Perhaps it was all in my head, but the pair looked somehow different. The old animosity and friction that had existed between them was erased; Olivia in particular, looked more comfortable than she had ever looked in his presence. Magic is a wonderful thing, but compared to the miraculous emotional transformations that sometimes happen between people, it pales.

During their meeting they decided that Olivia would spend more time with Sanjay—three days, to be precise. If she would tell me about those three days and give me permission, I would share more here; but the story of what happened during that time is hers alone. After the scroll investigations were settled, Spindlebrock promised us more time to pursue our adventure with Daksh, if we wished. No time was wasted in getting her set for the trip—this time she was excited to go!—and within an hour she was on her way.

"The tribunal found nothing of consequence," the professor informed me as we again waved goodbye to Olivia. "The absence of evidence is a major roadblock. You've noted that yourself, throughout this investigation. We reviewed the meager facts, watched the most relevant parts of the surveillance video, and revisited all parts of the Cascabela involved yet again—and still came up empty-handed. We might reasonably assume that ghosts were to blame, if not for the bit of glove material you found. Really, I believe that every angle has been examined, to no avail."

"So, the tribunal is complete then?"

"Well, all except a final report and formal disbanding. Each member must make a statement, and we have to catalog our findings—but in short, yes. The real work is over and done, almost as quickly as it started."

We had made our way inside, and took some seats in the lobby.

"The staff weren't much help to the tribunal, unfortunately; they're too overly cautious. Even though Lowen instructed them to give us their full cooperation, they were so reserved that we could barely get statements out of them. None of them remembered anything, if we're to take them at their word. Nothing notable happened that day, nothing was seen or heard. And, to be frank, I can understand their reservation."

"What do you mean?"

"I phoned Lewis and had him do deep background checks on everyone on staff the day of the theft—I went into our interviews with the intel he provided, in point of fact. Most of them have checkered pasts, and a few have alternate identities. I think that unscrupulous workers are a common feature of this industry, and that makes our work that much harder. They were probably scared to death of being considered as suspects."

Spindlebrock went quiet, and I debated in my head whether I should throw out my idea of interviewing Lowen and the inner chamber guard.

"It doesn't seem likely that the guards would stick around if they were involved," I said at length. "But that doesn't mean they wouldn't have anything valuable to contribute, if they would only cooperate. I was wondering actually, do you know which guard was on duty in the inner chamber? The one from the video?"

"Yes. That was Tamanna O'Dea. She's from Ireland. Her parents are friends of Lowen's family, and she intends to build a career in the hospitality industry. Her record, in contrast to many, is clean. Everything checks out with her, according to Lewis—which is probably why Lowen had her working in the inner chamber."

"Well—", I hesitated. "I know you've interviewed her already, and I know Lowen is busy, but—I'd like to sit down, the four of us, and go over it one more time."

"The four of us? You mean you, me, Lowen, and Tamanna?"

"Yes."

He thought for a few moments.

"We have the transcript of her interview, but I suppose that wouldn't do?"

My brain wouldn't let go of the idea that something more could come of meeting the guard myself. Spindlebrock saw it in my scrunched up face.

"OK, we'll revisit it all once more. Lowen can be difficult when he's busy and doesn't understand a demand on his time, but I do think you ought to meet him in any case. Give me a bit to round him up, explain things, and see if we can get Tamanna—we'll meet back here in the lobby this evening at six, and I'll let you know what I've come up with."

Chapter 9

This Changes Everything

I won't bore the reader with a detailed recounting of what I did while I waited for Spindlebrock to make arrangements with Lowen and the guard Tamanna, but it may make sense to reveal a habit that I had taken up after the events with Talbot, which I wrote about in my previous book. The reader will recall, perhaps, that through the medium of created works, I was able to both locate Spindlebrock as the author of the Little Blue Book of Traveling Spells, and find the young man named Talbot, who had been abducted. In the case of Talbot, he was located using a chess piece; in the case of Spindlebrock, a book. And there was, of course, Olivia's letter.

After those events unfolded and after I learned about Conexus and my affinity for it, I formed a habit without thinking, of touching random objects in my environment to see if they would trigger any response. It was a natural curiosity, I think. When I first realized I was doing it, the notion that perhaps I was being intrusive entered my mind. But I quickly came to terms with the fact that having gifts means using them, and in my case it meant becoming familiar with them. I've never intruded on anyone in this casual pursuit; when I've encountered objects that triggered the response, I've interacted with them only enough to examine my own abilities, without seeking to reveal identities or trespass on personal affairs.

I mention this now simply to point out that it had become, by this time, a subconscious behavior. So as I waited for Spindlebrock I went about the casino, casually exploring, and occasionally touching different objects that I came upon. I revisited the vaults and touched several of the displays. Most of them elicited some response, which did not surprise me—keep in mind that most of these were designed quite carefully by the owners of the artifacts, so as to protect their contents. The display that had held the scroll did in fact connect me with Spindlebrock; and here, I will note, I didn't mind lingering a little to check up on my friend. He was in no distress, that I could detect.

In the casino gaming rooms, I caught sight of a fascinating carved handle on one of the machines, which I touched. To my surprise, the owner felt quite near, and quite angry. Without meaning to intrude at all, my ears were attuned to two nearby employees who were quarreling, and I assumed that one of them must have carved it. This fascinated me, though it was of no real consequence then or thereafter. My exploration that day, in point of fact, yielded no great clues or insights, but I mention it because it was how I passed the time in question; and also to remind my readers of Conexus, which was to become a source of important information later on in this adventure.

Six o'clock did eventually roll around, and I found myself back in the lobby with Spindlebrock. He was upbeat, and informed me that we were to have dinner within the hour, with Lowen and Tamanna. We got ourselves cleaned up, and made our way to the dining area in the casino's main restaurant.

Lowen stood as we entered, and Tamanna awkwardly followed. Lowen was taller than I had expected, with light hair and a bright smile. I took him to be in his thirties. Tamanna was of that particular beauty that comes from the Celtic regions, with flowing coppery red hair quite past her shoulders, and delicate ivory skin, tinged with a blushing constellation of rose-spectrum, sun-soaked freckles.

I must confess that while I was not a bit surprised by Lowen apart from his height, I was considerably distracted by Tamanna. While a lovely lady might distract or disarm a young man for no other reason beyond the biological, this wasn't the experience that I was having; something about her both intrigued and alarmed me, though I could not at the time lay my finger on it.

After our introductions, and a few motions from Lowen toward the restaurant staff, we were seated. The meal and conversation started almost simultaneously.

"So," Lowen began, "I hear that you are quite the detective."

"Indeed," interrupted Spindlebrock. "He has had the opportunity to prove his abilities in several high-profit cases recently. There are few that can claim his gifts or abilities."

Still looking at me, Lowen continued.

"That's right. I think I recall first hearing your name, Mr. Martin, a few years back in some case of missing persons."

"Please, call me Thomas," I responded, perhaps a little too quickly, as I was anxious to speak for myself. "There were a number of college-age people who had been abducted. We were contacted by a friend of Spindlebrock's to help in a particular case, and that eventually led us to the culprits."

Here, Lowen seemed to lose interest.

"Yes, yes. I think I remember most of what was passed around in idle conversation. Spindlebrock, wasn't there another case, the arson case? That one hit closer to home—for me, at least."

"The Arson Triangle. One of the fires was in a hotel you owned, Lowen."

"It sure was. The building was completely destroyed. Which of course isn't a big deal—that's what insurance is for, right?—but I lost numerous personal items in my offices, because of that fire. So, thank you, Thomas, for putting a stop to that mess before it got any worse!"

I tried to interpose with some objection about how the very nuanced case had little to do with the loss of physical things, and more to do with the emotional impact it had on the magical commonality, but my commentary fell by the wayside when a server brought two cocktails and set them in front of Spindlebrock and me. Spindlebrock spoke.

"Oh, I forgot to tell you—Thomas doesn't drink, and I'm technically still on the tribunal. Water is probably best for both of us this evening."

Lowen apologized, but Spindlebrock shrugged it off; water was already on the table.

"Now, Thomas," continued Lowen, "what was it you wanted to discuss about the scroll investigation? Spindlebrock seemed to think gathering us all together was very important, but we've already gone over everything multiple times."

"Yes, well, I was wanting to—I guess I was wanting to speak in person to the people closest to this whole affair. It's different in person, than in videos and transcripts. You're all in the room now, you see."

"Sure. We have Spindlebrock, who represents the owner of the scroll; me as the proprietor of the place where the crime occurred; and of course Tamanna, as the guard who let it happen."

Here he turned hastily to Tamanna, who was audibly stunned by this brusque assignment of guilt.

"Not that I blame you—it doesn't appear that anyone could have stopped it. I just mean to say, that is perhaps how others might see it. Maybe that's how Thomas sees it?"

"Not at all," I replied. "Your summary is reasonable, Lowen, and it's reasonable to say that others might want to assign blame, but blame doesn't solve mysteries. Tamanna, I'm especially interested in hearing about what you experienced the morning after the scroll was stolen."

She gave an uneasy glance in Lowen's direction, who motioned for her to proceed.

"Well," she started, "I guess it wasn't that interesting. I don't have much to say about it. We were set up on our guard watches. They're usually pretty boring, mostly just a matter of keeping visitors in line. You know, 'Please don't touch the display' and all that. Things don't get stolen here, but we don't like having to constantly clean off fingerprints."

"That makes sense. I've already asked this of others, but I'll ask you as well—nothing was cleaned off the display after the crime was discovered, is that correct?"

"Of course not—there are protocols for a breach. We secured the area, marked it off, and waited."

"Good, very good. You were saying, about your guard watch duties that day?"

"Yes—well, I had just been moved into the inner chamber and was starting my rounds when I noticed that the scroll case look looked open."

"Looked open?" I interrupted. "Didn't you notice that it was definitely open?"

"I guess not—" she started to reply, but at that moment the food arrived, and our conversation was derailed as everything about our dinner was settled. No one seemed to recognize the fact that Tamanna's last assertion required followup, and so we ate while Lowen and Spindlebrock carried most of what was a rather banal conversation about the entertainment industry and Spindlebrock's recent studies. The "ghost hunting vacation" that Olivia and I had originally embarked on was brought up, and Lowen noted that several of his businesses benefited substantially from that particular market. In short, we made small talk.

The idea that Tamanna wasn't certain whether the scroll case was open gnawed at me all the while. How could she not see it for sure? How could she not notice, and who had been on duty there before she arrived? Looking back, it was probably a good thing that there was a pause in which I could let my thoughts take a more definite form.

"Thank you, Lowen, for that that delight!" Spindlebrock chimed as we all finished eating.

"Wait until you see what's for dessert," Lowen replied. But before he could beckon the wait staff, I spoke up.

"Tamanna, if you would, could you please explain how it was that you said you only thought the scroll case looked open? I'm not sure if I quite understand why you said it that way."

"I mean, I had only been working here for a week, everything still felt pretty new to me."

"A week?" Spindlebrock queried, leaning forward in his chair and glancing between Lowen and Tamanna.

"What do you mean, a week?" interjected Lowen, flustered. "Your record says you've been employed with me for almost three years!"

She looked confused.

"I'm sorry, I—no one asked me about that during the tribunal interviews, they just asked how long I had worked for you. I didn't know it was important. I thought everyone knew; I was transferred here."

"The tribunal will view this as an error, Lowen, a gross oversight," rejoined Spindlebrock, leaning back and shaking his head.

"It is an error. The tribunal reviewed the employment records, didn't they? Come to think of it, I reviewed them myself, I don't recall seeing anything about a transfer. But then again, I don't know much about the software we use, I hire people to manage that. I can't possibly keep track of particulars."

"We reviewed them, but certainly didn't see anything about a transfer. Why would that be missing?"

"Oh, I think I know what must have happened," continued Lowen, ignoring Spindlebrock's question at first. "I do recall hearing that we had some staff leave, a week or two before the crime. I bet the head of security transferred you in to take their place, Tamanna. Perhaps he forgot to note the transfer, and just re-assigned your work location in the computer? We'd probably have to have our database people get in there to see exactly what happened. Maybe the report needs to be modified so it automatically includes that information, or so that it's required when you make that kind of change."

He turned to Spindlebrock.

"Yes, I understand your concerns. The testimony and info I gave you and the tribunal wasn't complete, apparently. I apologize my friend, but it wasn't on purpose —like I said, I don't know much about the computer system, and as you well know I can't manage these sorts of things myself, not with the number of businesses I run. In any case, that was a week before the crime, I can hardly see how it could matter."

"You're great at running your businesses, Lowen, but you're no sort of detective. Ask Thomas, he'll tell you that all information surrounding a case like this is important, even the most minute facts."

Here Spindlebrock paused for a brief but thoughtful moment.

"But don't worry, I'm not sure it would even be helpful to bring this up to the tribunal at this point. As the owner, you're not in charge of the records, that's someone else's job. There's no reasonable way the tribunal would hold you accountable for the oversight. In any case, it would probably be a waste of time and needless frustration for everyone to worry about it. I'll figure it all out and smooth it over."

Much of the remaining conversation that evening I will omit, as it didn't yield much in the way of new information. Lowen and Tamanna were helpful, and it was a pleasure to share an excellent meal, but my mind was fixated on the two new facts that had now been revealed: That there had been a recent change in the organization of in the guards—a fact that somehow seemed crucial to me, though I couldn't exactly tell why—and, that Tamanna was unsure about the scroll case being open or not.

At our parting, Lowen shook my hand and thanked me for my help.

"I'm not sure what else we can do, but if you need anything at all just let me know."

As we clasped hands, something in his eyes changed, as if he had a sudden inspiration.

"Thomas Martin... you know what? I recall overhearing a conversation at a hotel I own in Tahiti. They were talking about that case with the abductions, the one we talked about earlier, you know? As I recall, they mentioned that you had some kind of rare gift—confectus, or perplexis, or something like that—my Latin is terrible. Can you tell me about that? I've always been a bit curious about inborn magical talents, working as I do in the entertainment industry."

"Another time, Lowen," Spindlebrock interjected. "It's getting late, am I'm afraid the jet lag is still causing us some trouble. Plus, I need to wrap up my report and get it behind me."

Lowen looked disappointed, but we parted with promises on both sides, to do whatever we could to help.

Spindlebrock's comment about jet lag was more true than I wanted to admit, and we retired without much conversation. He was missing from the room when I awoke the next day, but caught up with me after breakfast.

"Thomas, good morning! Now that you've eaten, let's take a drive. I want to hear what thoughts you have about our dinner last night."

He had arranged a vehicle for us to use, a sturdy off-road type that looked something like a Land Rover. It was the first time I had been away from the Cascabela since arriving there, and I was glad for the change. As we approached the main road that would take us down the mountain, Spindlebrock turned uphill instead.

"I thought—" I began, but stopped myself when I realized that I really didn't have much to say. I had thought we were going to get away from the mountain and the casino, but it was clear that he had other ideas. After a pause, he filled in what was in my mind.

"That it would be nice to get away from all this for a bit, and explore the countryside. I agree with that, but there's a view I wanted to show you, and I didn't want to go too far today. I just wanted to get away from the hotel, so we could discuss things in peace—without any chance of being heard, I mean."

The road up the mountain became rough. It ended in a small clearing near the top where we parked. A path led the rest of the way up the mountain to the peak.

"We can walk a little, Thomas, it'll do us good."

The mountain where the Cascabela lies is not particularly impressive, except for the fact that it is the only high feature on an otherwise flat piece of landscape. Not a range of mountains like those further east, it is a single conical feature, high and steep enough to look imposing with nothing adjacent to lend competition to the sight. The peak is barren rock, while most of the mountain below is covered in jungle-forest woods.

We walked to the summit. The path was easy enough—in fact, the only difficulty was a rather large snake that we came across, sunning itself. It was far enough away when we saw it that we weren't in any danger, even if it was venomous; but Spindlebrock reacted so quickly at the sight of it, pulling his wand from concealment and sending it flying through the air, that I didn't have time to even try to identify it. Though I have no particularly acute fear of snakes, my heart was pounding from the suddenness of it all.

Spindlebrock, of course, was not phased.

"When in the jungle, I clear away snakes first and ask questions later. Better safe than sorry, as they say. Well, here we are. It's not Mount Everest, of course, but the view is nice. To the east you can see the area where Sanjay lives—that jungle and mountain range, over there in the distance. But what I wanted to show you was the casino, from another vantage point."

My eyes followed his finger down the mountain. The Cascabela was looming, oddly quite visible through the thick trees.

"Huh. I thought we'd only see a bit of the roof, to be honest."

"From here, you can see quite a bit, because of the riverbed path. It creates a wash, a sort of natural break or thinning in the canopy."

I recalled the riverbed that had been so interesting to me the day before.

"That's right! We saw Daksh in a riverbed. I followed the path of it, and it seemed like it would have led directly under the casino, if they hadn't diverted it."

"Indeed, it used to run under the casino. Well, back then it wasn't a casino at all. And I say that it would run, but it would only trickle at best—except when it rained."

I looked at him for more of an explanation. His eyes were fixed on the building.

"I've read," he continued, "that the oldest part of the building was already there when this area was settled—and in India, that's a long, long time ago. Before that, no one knows anything about it. In the eighteen hundreds, apparently, a new structure was built up around it by a wealthy British family—a magical family. In that time period, the water flowed here year round from a spring, and it flooded only in the monsoons. They were the ones who originally built the channels that would divert the floodwaters. The concrete spillways were added later."

Here Spindlebrock shook his gaze from the building and changed the subject.

"Now, tell me what you thought of our dinner last night. That's the main reason I wanted to come up here."

"Well," I said, composing myself, "I still think that it's odd that Tamanna didn't say that she noticed the scroll case was open, only that it looked as if it might be open."

"And why does that detail bother you?"

"It seems to me that she should have known right away whether it was open or closed. She should have been more definite."

"Perhaps, but by her own admission, she really hadn't spent much time looking at it. She was, as we learned, rather new at the Cascabela."

"That's the other thing that bothered me. She was new, didn't have much knowledge of the items she was guarding, and only had a vague suspicion that the case was opened, not a definite recognition. If she didn't walk in, make her rounds, and spot the problem right away, then it makes it very difficult for us to pinpoint when it was actually opened, and when the scroll disappeared. She could have missed it before that morning. Do you see what I mean?"

Spindlebrock began to pace, as he does when new thoughts are rolling into his mind.

"Yet," he said, "the burglar was caught on camera the evening before, so doesn't that secure a definite window for the crime?"

I was about to give my thoughts on the subject, but he answered his own question.

"It doesn't! We've connected the video footage of the burglar from the night before, with Tamanna noticing the open case the following morning. This made sense, until we learned that Tamanna was new, and knew very little about the object she was guarding. She didn't know for certain that the case was opened, she only thought it might be, just as you so keenly noted! How did you realize that detail was so vital?"

Again, I didn't have time to interject before he carried on.

"It is therefore possible that the case was opened and the scroll removed before that night. And if Tamanna didn't really know what she was looking at, did any of the others? Perhaps no one noticed. Or, perhaps they were so accustomed to their job, they didn't really even look at the scroll case. Did she only say something because she was new? Maybe the others—the ones with more to hide—didn't want to say anything and be blamed? This could potentially change everything."

"I agree. I think we need to review the security video again, and look back even further. Maybe even back to before she was transf—"

My mouth froze agape mid-word. Spindlebrock stopped pacing and looked at me.

"What? What is it?"

"She—it's—"

He watched me intently, waiting for me to gather my wits. I had mentioned to the reader that when I first saw Tamanna, something about her unsettled me. In this moment, I realized what it was.

"I just realized something—Evalyn. Tamanna looked like Evalyn!"

Chapter 10

A Very Old Friend

I t was jarring to suddenly realize why I had been so distracted by Tamanna the previous evening. I had only seen Evalyn a few times in connection with the case with the abductions, but her impression on my mind was deep; not because she was beautiful, thought that was true. Mostly, the impression she left was from the interview I had with her at Bardo's, which ended with a handshake that knocked me unconscious, and which to this day makes my hand burn when I recollect it.

Before I realized what was going on, Spindlebrock had rushed us back to our vehicle without a word. He started to speak once we were inside.

"Everything indeed has changed. This is serious. We can't continue on like this, not without knowing for sure. When you say she looked like Evalyn, how much like her, would you say?"

I recalled that Spindlebrock had only briefly encountered Evalyn, on the bridge when the whole group of Crane's abductees was rescued.

"Pretty similar."

"Was it her? Is that at all possible?"

"No—she looked like her, but it definitely wasn't her. There were differences, certainly. But I think that from a distance I could mistake the two. Or maybe—"

"Maybe on a security recording, you could mistake the two."

"That's just what I was thinking! I knew something was wrong with that video of the inner vault, it bothered me in the back of my mind somewhere. I really want to watch that footage one more time. I wasn't thinking about anyone in those videos being someone I might know."

Spindlebrock tapped the steering wheel.

"Do you understand what this could mean?"

I only had vague, foreboding notions.

"Not entirely," I confessed.

"If Evalyn is connected to this affair at all—if there's even a chance that she's connected—then Crane is likely to be connected as well. His involvement is something I've feared from the beginning. How's your acting?"

He turned to me. My face felt ghost white and frozen.

"Not good, as usual. You really need to work on that. But never mind, we'll just have to stick together. We're going back, and we don't want to reveal anything to anyone."

"What do you mean?"

"Well, we have several loose ends to tie up, and those must be addressed at the Cascabela. There's the tribunal, the reports, and the insight about Tamanna—I mean, the insight that she was transferred. It would look very odd if we didn't follow that up. And yet, we don't want to dig around too frenetically."

He could see that I still didn't quite understand his trepidation.

"If Crane is involved, then Crane is most certainly watching. Perhaps he has other spies—he certainly has a way with convincing people to do his bidding. At this point, we can't trust our landscape of investigative leads; we must review everything. But we have to be careful so as not to reveal that we directly suspect that Crane or Evalyn are involved in any of this."

"But, why would Crane be watching at the Cascabela? He has what he wants, doesn't he. And Evalyn left a week ago."

"Right. But Crane is a chess player, I think. He will be watching, you can guarantee it—he'll be doing all that he can to understand our move, so that he can plan his next move. We can't let him know that we've discovered him already, even if all we have is a vague suspicion and a potential risk."

"So, what do we do?"

As we started back toward the casino, Spindlebrock laid out his plan. We would return and revisit the case, holding off on any new lines of inquiry. He would finish his report, and help to close the tribunal. In two days, when Olivia was to return, Spindlebrock would announce our disappointing failures very publicly to Lowen, and the three of us would depart presumably for Sanjay's to continue the original purpose of our trip, the pursuit of the supernatural. That would be the official story, as is said; but rather than go to Sanjay's, we would continue our scroll investigation remotely, with aid and methods that Spindlebrock would reveal to when it became expedient.

The plan seemed reasonable, and though I was skeptical concerning Olivia's cooperation, Spindlebrock wasn't in the mood for deliberation. As he was the one holding the steering wheel, we made our way back to the hotel.

The next two days were slow and stressful (a horrid combination, as those familiar will understand), and so I'll spare the reader a detailed outline. All you need to know is that we reviewed the case without making any new effort that might expose our position, then we re-connected with Olivia (who was, in fact, very willing to acquiesce to the professor's plan), and departed from the Cascabela without incident.

Rather than hiring a driver, Spindlebrock had a car delivered directly to the hotel; not a rental car, but the personal vehicle of an unknown friend. It was small and a little beat up, but it had wonderfully concealing tint on the windows, and it certainly wouldn't stand out on the streets in that region. As it carried us away from the casino—once again with Spindlebrock at the wheel—Olivia and I both queried the professor about our next destination.

"Before we talk about that, let me show you a little something."

He fished in his pocket while darting around a pair of disorderly scooters. Eventually, an outstretched palm displayed a small black box.

"Thomas, you remember when Lewis showed us that map, where he was measuring magical energy in Phoenix?"

"Sure."

"This is one of the latest of his magical sensors."

I eyed the black box.

"And? Will this help us find the scroll?"

"No, but while I'm here in India I told him I'd place a few sensors for him. He's building quite a network for his next project."

He pocketed the cube and returned both hands to the steering wheel.

"As for our current destination; we're headed to a temple."

"A temple?"

"Yes that's right, a temple. They dot the landscape in this part of the world; for many reasons, I think. A friend oversees this particular temple. We need somewhere safe to disappear to for a bit, and it's the safest place I can think of. While we're there, I'll place one of the sensors in it—two birds with one stone, as it were."

"But first," he continued, "we need to make sure that we're not being followed."

Whether it was from real necessity, or some actual perceivable threat, I do not know; but Spindlebrock took us on the most chaotic and circuitous drive imaginable through the environs of Salem. Farm, forest, hill, jungle, and city were all traversed in rapid succession, with never a dead-end or any apparent unexpected turn. In fact, looking back I think there was hardly even a stop, whether sign or light demanded it or not. He seemed to have an exhaustive knowledge of the area.

When I had almost given up on us ever reaching any destination, we rounded a curve in a remote area and came all at once upon a temple. To my surprise, it was abuzz with visitors. I wondered aloud if we would be able to discreetly find a place to hide in such a busy building.

"Not the quickest route, but it certainly eliminates any possibility of being followed. Leave you bags here, we'll get them later."

He shepherded us to the entrance of the temple, where we fell in behind another group of tourists. We moved as they moved, all the while Spindlebrock pointing out features of the temple and explaining history and religious practice as if a temple tour was his intention from the beginning.

We finally came to a place of offering. To this day I can't figure out how he did it, but with our heads turned for a fraction of a second, he produced three bunches of bananas, handing one to each of us.

"Here, take these. Follow me closely, but don't say anything."

In a fit of uncharacteristic cultural carelessness, Spindlebrock spun around and proceeded to bypass all the people who were moving quietly through the line to set their offerings down. He approached a man who was directing the visitors.

"Excuse me? You there! We have to get going, but we want to leave these. Is that alright?"

Without waiting for the director to respond, he started to move toward the shrine.

The man looked alarmed.

"Wait! Sir, you must wait!"

"No, it's alright, we're not staying. We just need to set these down and leave."

As the director attempted to place himself between Spindlebrock and the shrine, the professor darted from side to side as if intent on ignoring him. I tried to follow, and Olivia just watched in horror. After some moments, two particularly large men came into the room and hurried over to our group. One of the men took the bananas from each of us in turn, handing them to the bewildered director, while the other used his body to deflect Spindlebrock into a corner. The man who had retrieved the bananas then rounded Olivia and me into the same corner.

"Sir," the larger of the two said, "if you'll please go this way, we can direct you back to the parking."

He motioned to a hallway at the back of the room. The guards followed behind us as Spindlebrock led the way. We went through a series of passages, and arrived at an old door. I noted two things. First, that the door wasn't average in any sense; it was quite old and of some rich jungle wood, with course, fast-growing grains worn smooth by the polish of centuries, and an ornate sliding brass bar lock. A key was already in the opening. The second thing I noticed was that the guards did not move to open the door, but let us approach it on our own, turning their backs on us and stepping away.

"Listen and watch closely, both of you. Commit this to memory," the professor whispered as he reached for the key.

A muttered but audible incantation followed, accompanied by a most peculiar manipulation of the key in specific rotations. This was immediately followed by a most satisfying "click" of the lock mechanism, a sliding of the brass bar, and a noiseless opening of the door inward into a dark, cavernous void. Without another word from us or the guards, we entered, and the door shut behind us on its own. Before anyone could say a thing, a tall elderly Indian woman emerged from the darkness in the hall before us. She was shrouded in what looked like yard upon yard of sumptuous traditional Indian textiles. A light seemed to emanate from the folds as she approached.

"Noooo," she said, slowly shaking her head and drawing out her voice. "Do not bow. This is not the way to worship the Siddhar."

She stopped a couple yards away. We stood, transfixed.

"In Paramavadhi, I have seen you coming. Your offering is accepted, though this man did offend in bringing it."

She nodded toward Spindlebrock. Her eyes were closed, and her hands, which had been at her sides, were now brought before her in what I later learned is called Anjali Mudra, or simply "prayer hands."

The professor slowly pulled out his wand. With a flick of his wrist he produced a puff of air and swept away her flowing outer layers—including a beautiful davani-shawl—

revealing a powered-on flashlight tucked into a band wrapped around her waist.

Her eyes opened, and she smiled mischievously.

"Cyrus Cardamom Spindlebrock, what kind of manners are these to show your guru?"

This was the first time I had ever heard someone address Spindlebrock by his full name. Even those closest to him generally called him by his last name only, or by "C.C." on rarer occasions. I had, at times, doubted his initials actually stood for anything at all.

The professor smiled and slowly put away his wand, before reaching out and taking both the woman's hands in his. He spoke softly, with a fondness that bordered on reverence.

"Karthika, it is very good to see you again, but you should turn down the satire. These guests are not tourists. This girl is a pupil of Sanjay."

Karthika's beaming face dropped instantly to a stony level of seriousness that seemed ill-fitted to her buoyant external character. She dropped her hands once more to her side, stepped slightly back, and eyed Olivia up and down. Her gaze then turned to me.

"And the boy?"

"He is my pupil."

The old woman smiled again as Spindlebrock introduced us.

"Oh, Cyrus, I didn't think—but this is wonderful news. Come, all three of you, and we will go where we might talk."

With an upward flick of one finger, this fascinating apparition turned on an unseen light switch somewhere, illuminating the hall. I saw that the corridor terminated in what appeared to be solid stone, a short distance away. With the light on, I could see Karthika better. Her age was difficult to surmise; she was youthful in smile and spirit, in appearance between fifty and seventy depending on her expression. She was tall and handsome, with ebony-black, satin-smooth hair pulled back in a ponytail.

She turned and walked toward the stone wall with alarming speed. Just as she was about to crash into the rock, she threw one hand in a wide arc, and the stone slid aside as if it were weightless. As we all passed through the opening, I saw that the stone wall she had just moved was at least six feet thick.

The chamber we entered was unlit, and remained so until we were all inside and the stone blockade replaced with another sweep of the arm. By the glow of her little waistband flashlight, I could see Karthika remotely flick another unseen switch with a movement of her finger, and the room was revealed by high hanging lamps.

We had entered what looked like a cave. The ceiling was domed, of solid rock, and perhaps twenty feet high in the center. The circular cavern was divided into four distinct areas. First, the entrance, notable only for its empty space. This was connected to a sitting area, with couches and chairs and a small round table, and what looked like a place for preparing food and drink. Further on there were desks with computers and monitors, with one large screen mounted to the stone behind and above. Beyond the desks was a screened area with hints of a bedroom just discernible. Besides the stone door we had just used, there appeared to be no other way in or out.

"Well? What do you think about what I've done with the place?"

Spindlebrock beamed as he looked around.

"Aside from the computers, it hasn't changed a bit."

Our host sighed, ushered us hastily to the sitting area, then busily started preparing tea. Cups, plates, and supplies moved through the air around her as she rifled through a small cabinet.

"You're telekinetic?" I inquired.

"Yes, dear," she replied without lifting her head.

"I haven't heard a thing from or about Professor Harris for some time now," she continued, looking over her shoulder at Spindlebrock as she floated a diffuser full of leaves into a pot of hot water.

Spindlebrock cleared his throat.

"Well, she's been very busy. What with her daughter, and school—and I've been busy, too."

"Oh?"

"Absolutely. Thomas and I have saved the world at least half a dozen times in the last few years."

She chuckled.

"For instance," he continued unruffled, "there was a case of missing persons. They were all college age kids, Delphine's daughter among them. Thomas, tell her all about it, from the very beginning in the bookshop."

Deflecting her attention, the professor walked me through a very detailed re-telling of my adventures with his Little Blue Book. Karthika listened intently as she served us all tea. When I got to the part about Olivia, she seemed quite surprised.

"You mean, that terrible man abducted you—and now you're here?"

"Yes," whispered Olivia. The story seemed to have a peculiar effect on her.

"And do you have any notion as to why he abducted you?" our host persisted.

Olivia started to breathe quick and shallow. Karthika took a seat opposite her.

"I don't remem—" she started, but she couldn't catch her breath.

"You don't remember. But it seems to me that you want to remember, is that right?"

Olivia scanned the old woman's face imploringly, but did not answer.

"Don't be alarmed, young woman. This is a good place for remembering."

As I watched Olivia closely, concerned that she might faint, something about her changed. At first I thought I had something in my eyes, and I attempted to rub them. But it was still there, a fuzziness around her, almost like a light or a faintness that I couldn't comprehend at first. Then I realized she was becoming ever so slightly transparent.

Knowing that I was sure to rush to her at any moment, Spindlebrock put his hand on my chest and whispered, "Wait. She'll be alright."

Chapter 11

Muddled Memories

Karthika placed a steadying hand on Olivia's arm, and sat quietly with her for a few moments.

"You are Sanjay's student—so there is probably a small stone in your pocket. Take it out."

She obeyed, her face the very picture of pleading and shock. Karthika spoke to her softly and soothingly.

"Calm yourself and try to breathe regularly. There is no danger and no rush here. Breathe. Follow my breaths."

She opened her hands upward and breathed methodically, motioning for Olivia to do the same. With some coaching, in a mixture of words and terms I understood and some that were entirely foreign to me, she succeeded in calming Olivia.

"That is good. Now, place the stone on the table before you. Very good. Repeat after me."

As the two spoke their incantations, Spindlebrock and I listened and watched. It's difficult to entirely describe what I saw, beyond what I shared about the fuzziness of her appearance; only, the odd aspect that seemed to change Olivia now also changed the old woman.

After some minutes, the pair slowly began appearing more and more defined, until they looked entirely normal. They both exhaled deeply, and opened their eyes. Olivia also opened her fist, which had been at her side. Another stone, slightly lighter in tone than the one on the table, was in her palm.

"Thank you."

Olivia was breathing calmly. Karthika touched her arm and smiled.

"I'm so glad to be able to show you something in this place. Sanjay must be very proud, you're doing well. How long have you been his pupil?"

"Well—he and I only just met a few days ago."

"I see."

A shadow of thoughtfulness crossed the worn face, and for a time we were all quiet. Then, she turned to Spindlebrock.

"It seems you've not lost your gift of finding peculiar talent. I can tell you what Sanjay perhaps has not; this girl will change the magical world."

"With my help, of course," was his reply.

"Yes, dear, with your help."

With this opening, Professor Spindlebrock took the opportunity to invite Olivia to share, with his usual modicum of tact, what it was that she had been trying to recall. She volunteered that a memory of her time under Crane's control had inexplicably come back to her mind, but that the memory was foggy and unclear. It was a memory that she had recalled more than once, without ever being able to get anything more out of it.

The reader will perhaps remember that Olivia, at the close of the affair with the abductions, had been rescued without consuming a memory-destroying Mundus potion, and that we had learned that she had only interacted with Crane in person once, when they first met. At the time, Spindlebrock tried to get details from her about his appearance, his personality, or whatever he could think of, but her memory was so faded that we were sure some manipulation had occurred. It was, for us, a dead end.

"This always bothered me," Olivia explained as we drank our tea.

"I could recall meeting him, and talking with him, but I couldn't remember anything specific. Like, where we met, or why I even met with him in the first place. I've really wanted to know how I could have gotten mixed up with such a—person like that.

"And when we got here, I started to remember again, and this nervous energy took over, like an anxiety attack. It wasn't until Karthika helped me—well, she cleared things up for me, I think."

"How? What did you see? What did you learn?" pursued the professor.

She looked at Karthika, as if asking permission to share. The woman smiled at her and spoke softly.

"A few days is not enough time to teach someone so young about something so immense. But let me tell you this once and for all: If your heart wishes to share anything with anyone, then you may. Only know that people can understand what they are able to understand, you can't pour knowledge into them. And since you are young, and inexperienced, it is even harder, because the knowledge is being soaked up by thirsty ground inside you. It is soaked up, not overflowing yet. Share when you want, you need no permission, but be patient with yourself and others."

Olivia nodded, closed her eyes, and breathed deeply for several moments before continuing.

"With Karthika's help, I re-visited my first encounter with Crane. It felt like a vision or a dream, I guess, but I think we actually visited some place, or some time, in my memories. Like we were actually there, watching it unfold.

"I really wanted to see his face, to remember what he looked like. I know it's important to you both, to know who he is. And I think it would bring closure in my heart too, to know.

"But, I was disappointed. I recall perfectly now, that day I met him. Another student at the school, from one of my classes, bumped into me when I was off-campus at work. He told me that there was a magician who had some information—I was studying ghosts, even back then—that I would be interested in. I couldn't resist, and since it was a friend of a friend sort of thing, I didn't think anything about whether it would be safe or not.

"Anyway, we met at a restaurant. Crane was in a back room—I went to see him with my friend, all three of us. His name was Norman Collins, I remember now—my friend, that is. It was him. I actually never saw or thought of him after the abduction, I think that was on purpose. I think he lured me there."

"I've never heard the name," interjected Spindlebrock, "but I'll certainly look into it when we return to the university."

"Thank you. Well, we went back to see Crane, and he was sitting at a table. His clothing looked archaic, a brown monastic cloak with the hood drawn. I thought he was odd, but then I'm not worried about people being odd, and so it didn't bother me. Magicians can be extremely odd, as you know.

"At the time, when this actually happened, I could see his face. I remember that I could. It wasn't like he was hiding —or at least it didn't seem like it to me. But in my memory, and even in this vision where I could see so much more, his face was still somehow hidden. I mean, it wasn't obscured, but I couldn't see it. I'm not sure how to explain it."

"A cloak, you say? Fascinating."

Spindlebrock stood and began to pace.

"Please, go on."

"Well, the memory continued. He spoke to me about my interest in ghosts, some things about elemental magic, and about my schooling. He said he could help me discover the truth, and find the answers I was seeking. I was about to ask him a few questions, when a server arrived with drinks."

"Of course," laughed the professor. "A man of potions is always ready to offer a drink."

"I didn't know that he was 'a man of potions' at the time; in my memory I watched myself drink, unaware. The vision changed."

"How so?"

"I don't know how to describe it. Almost like looking at a color photo, then suddenly there's a filter over your vision and you're looking at sepia tone. Except it's not really the color that you see that has changed, but the feeling. Does that make sense?"

"It makes enough sense. Please, continue. I'll not interrupt again until you're through."

Olivia finished her description of the vision. Through it she learned that after giving her that first potion, Crane had manipulated her into helping him. He promised to help her, but proceeded to artificially create in her a great empathy for his "cause," as he described it. She was led to believe, in her altered state, that he was working to liberate young people in the magical commonality, and to overcome some perceived but never explained injustice by building a group that could create a new commonality. He needed her, begged her to help him lead this effort.

It was all still somewhat unclear to her, but this vision shed more light on that part of her life than she had been able to find up to that point; and it brought her a great deal of comfort to see herself, and know that she acted as best as she could given the circumstances. She was at peace with the memory.

"So, he's a radical who wants to rebuild our magical society. Very interesting. Did he ever stand, while you were with him?" queried the professor.

"No."

"And so, we can't even guess his height. I suppose his build was something of a mystery as well, with the cloak."

"He was an average sort of build."

"Yes, the laws of the universe would tend toward an average it seems. Well, then all we really have to go off—in terms of us getting any new clue as to Crane's identity from your memory, I mean to say—is that cloak. What I wouldn't give for my library right now!"

"How could that help?" I interjected.

"There's a volume titled, Magical Objects: A Catalog, by Marcus Saunders. He was an Irish magician, seventeenth century, but his book was widely translated, updated, and re-published, until the early nineteenth century."

"And this cloak, you think it would be in there?"

"It's possible. It certainly sounds like a rather notable magical object, and I somehow feel like I've heard of it before; a cloak that can obscure memory."

Spindlebrock stopped his pacing and looked at the ceiling of the cave, lost in thought.

"Mother! Do you—"

Here he paused and looked at Olivia and me, an expression of mild discomfort on his face.

"I sometimes call her that," he explained, "because I've known her since I was a child. Karthika, do you have a library here?"

This question shocked me more than his use of the word mother. I looked around me for something I might have missed in our surroundings, a bookcase, door, or anything that could hold even the smallest library. I saw nothing.

"Of course I do."

"And do you have a copy of Saunders in it? Could we look?"

"I think so. But—do you really think it's wise? Now?"

She was motioning toward us.

"Yes, yes. I'll explain later, but there's nothing that I know, or that you know, that I want to keep from Thomas and Olivia."

"I see. You used to be a man of such impenetrable secrets, Cyrus. I'm glad you're opening up. Well, then follow me, all of you."

We arose, and walked to the middle of the cavern. In the center of the floor was what looked like a Zen garden (for lack of a better comparison) consisting of neatly raked gravel, set into a depression in the stone floor. Spindlebrock examined it approvingly.

"You're so tidy! Mine always looks like a country road, strewn about haphazard."

"I'm sure that's so, dear. Now, stand back everyone."

She produced a wand with surprising speed, and started into a complicated charm that sounded vaguely familiar.

Suddenly and without warning, a filing cabinet sprung up in the middle of the Zen garden.

Olivia and I gasped and almost tripped, stumbling backward.

"It's like the luggage!" I exclaimed, recalling that I had heard a similar charm before, on the streets of Adana. Karthika looked indignant.

"Luggage? Who ever heard of such a thing?"

Spindlebrock coughed.

"It was one time. The situation demanded it—it was really quite dire. Apart from that, I only use the charm you taught me in the absolute privacy of my File Room, of course."

The reader will hopefully forgive me for spending a fair amount of writing on what seem like trivial details. By this point in time, much of the magical world no longer surprised me the way it did at first. But looking back I realize that these few happenings were small system shocks, reminding me that I hadn't yet seen all that there was to see.

The rocks in the Zen garden were, as you may have guessed, magically condensed cabinets, full of books, papers, scrolls, and all manner of magical records, cleverly concealed. The garden of stones was in fact her library—her equivalent of Spindlebrock's File Room. I had seen such magic but once to that point, used to secure some luggage during an exploration; it was during a time of so much activity that I hardly recalled it until that point. I later learned that this particular and powerful charm was known only to the professor and Karthika. It was, in fact, Karthika who invented it.

Witnessing the memory recalling event with Olivia and Karthika was surreal, and even though Olivia had already shared the details of her previous, semi-related Sanjay experiences, nothing is as potent in recital as it is in plain view. My head was swirling with new information, new experiences, and as-yet unresolved mysteries. I stood by, astonished and overwhelmed, as Karthika expanded and shrank her personal library in search of the volume that Spindlebrock sought. When she found it and the Zen garden was restored, I burst out in a flood of questions. Spindlebrock ushered us back to the sitting area, set down the book, asked Karthika to fix another round of a more relaxing tea, and took it upon himself to respond.

"I'm sorry Thomas, you certainly deserve more information—as do you, Olivia. Well, let's start with this room. I told you that we needed someplace safe to hide, and that was true. What I didn't tell you is that we would be using one of the most secure safe rooms known to man or magician."

"What makes it so secure?"

"The fact that we're under several meters of solid granite, with the largest opening no larger than the diameter of a liter bottle of soda—for starters."

"A bottle of soda?"

"That's all it takes to vent and return the air, and bring in other needed utilities."

"What about the door we came through?"

"The door opens onto a short passage, which you saw, terminating in nothing but solid granite behind the door. The entire cave was carved from that door inward."

Olivia and I looked at one another.

"Yes, yes. When we came through it, it opened in the temple above us on the surface."

"You're saying," I ventured, "that it's a sort of portal?"

"That's an apt enough description. It's called a Selectivam Ostium—a selective doorway."

"How does it work?"

"That is a much more complicated question—do you mind if I answer your other simpler questions first, before we address that? If we don't, we may never come back to them."

I nodded.

"Wonderful. What was the next in your barrage?"

He was referencing the flood of questions that I had started with. He continued before I could recall the order myself.

"Oh yes, that's right, you wanted to know about the magical properties of this room; but let's add that to the question about the Selectivam Ostium, because the answer is related. Let's see, after that it was something about our plans for the scroll, right? Well, as you can see, part of that bottle-sized opening is used for networking cables and power—we have a pretty secure computer setup right over there, put together by some of the best magical hackers in the world. I mean, they're hackers, and they're magical, not that they're using magic for hacking. Like Lewis, guys like him."

Spindlebrock thought.

"In fact, I think he might have consulted with them. Anyway, it doesn't matter. Talent. Pure, raw talent. And we get to benefit from it. We'll use the system over there, with Lewis remotely helping, to get all the info we need to aid us in our scroll investigation."

"One thing we needed, I think, was more time at the Cascabela. I really wanted to re-watch all those video feeds."

"And you shall, Thomas, you shall."

"How?"

"I don't know, I only know that I requested as much from Lewis, and he has never failed me. So, on to the next question, or we'll never get back to the fun and interesting stuff. What was the next thing? I've quite forgotten."

I had forgotten as well, but with some back and forth he helped me feel more calm about our situation, and we eventually returned to the subject of the Selectivam Ostium and the cave. He was right about it being a most interesting subject.

"As I said before, the cave was built around the door. The door came first, you see. It was built directly above the cave, in the temple. It wasn't built for any special purpose, it was just one of the doors in the temple, actually. But it just happened to be perfectly placed for the charm, and so it was enchanted for the purpose it serves now, as a Selectivam Ostium."

"Who enchanted it? You?" asked Olivia.

"I don't know who—and I don't know how they did it either. These things happened long ago, and the magicians who performed the feats didn't see fit to preserve the knowledge or pass it on. I've had to find out many of these sorts of things through careful searching and study."

Karthika had rejoined us and was sitting and sipping her drink quietly as we held ours. Spindlebrock addressed her.

"You do have the maps still, don't you? I know we were just in the library, but could we retrieve those too?"

She looked stunned.

"They are not kept in the library," she said quietly. "But I will get them. It will only take me a few moments."

She went to the stone barricade, swiped it aside with a movement of her arm, disappeared into the corridor and shut it behind her. When she was gone, Spindlebrock spoke quickly.

"You two don't realize it, but this visit is very hard on her. It's out of the ordinary in many ways. You'll forgive her if she doesn't immediately warm up to you. I'm not sure if she really understands—or maybe believes—what I'm doing."

"That's easy to grasp," answered Olivia. "Since we rarely understand what you're doing either."

Her old sarcasm was tempered by a playful tone and a warm smile.

"That's true. Very true. Soon though. You'll all understand soon enough."

Before we could finish our drinks, the rock was sliding again. Karthika stood before us, a collection of scrolls under one arm.

"And," she said to Spindlebrock, "you intend to show them these, do you?"

"Yes."

"Then what? You're going to erase these poor kids memories, is that it?"

"No, mother, wait—"

"Don't you mother me, Cyrus. Did you drag these two all the way down here, to use them for something? Yet another one of your endless pursuits?"

"Of course not, I—"

"Well then what? What is it?"

"If you'll—"

"Forget it! I don't want to know! You've done many things in your life, young man, many bad things that I'm not proud to know about. When will it all end?"

Spindlebrock's mouth hung open, devoid of any response. He looked sincerely injured. He cleared his throat, wiped his eyes, and looked at the floor. No one spoke for several minutes. Finally, he whispered.

"It has ended already, mother. That's why we're here."

Chapter 12

Maps, Answers, and More Questions

All of this was, for me at the time, cryptic, emotionally charged, and uncomfortable. The two shared a long gaze, then a few whispered words that I could not make out; Karthika's face softened, and we all moved on. The maps that Karthika had procured were set carefully on the couch, where Spindlebrock examined them and selected one. The map was unrolled on the small round table, as we looked on with rapt interest.

It was ancient in every sense, drawn with dark, uneven inks on an animal skin scroll. Before Spindlebrock spoke, the only thing I understood from examining it was that the map was of the Ottoman Empire, Arabia, Persia, and India. In the margins were notes in a variety of obscure and unrecognizable languages.

"This is the base of the first series of maps. These are very old, and unique in the world, and so I'll ask you both to please not touch them. Karthika, do you have any small weights?"

She nodded, and moments later a small vase full of smooth glass pebbles floated over and set itself down by the map. Spindlebrock removed a handful and placed one on each corner of the map to hold it in place.

"The writing you may ignore for now, but take note of our general location here in southern India"

He indicated a region on the map. It was marked with several X's of various sizes, in red and black ink.

"Now, let's add another layer."

From the pile, he selected and unrolled another scroll. This one was of a very thin, flexible, translucent velum. He placed it over the first map, and secured it with more weights. Though it was faded yellow with age, you could make out the thick, dark lines of the map below it. On this overlay were regions outlined in graphite, large swooping rivers of gray, and tendrils as of smaller creeks and washes.

"This is a strata—I call it Strata Temporis. It will mean nothing to you, perhaps. We'll add another layer."

He added another, similar in material and workmanship to the first, except that the designs scrawled on it were different.

"Strata Spatium."

"Time and Space," declared Olivia as she examined the map and its two layers.

"Correct, and simple enough. What do you make of it, Thomas?"

Combined, the three maps made quite a confusing mess. I studied them for several minutes, during which time no one said a thing. Then, it hit me.

"Confluences! Here, and here!"

I pointed to two large red X's.

"Look how these two rivers flow together, with the large red X at the outlet—the very definition of a confluence. This is where modern-day Adana is, if I'm not mistaken."

"Modern and ancient Adana", he corrected. "It has had that name for thousands of years. But you are right; that is Adana, home to one of the most potent confluences on the planet."

"And what are these X's dotting the south of India?" Olivia asked.

"Let me show you—just one moment."

He removed the glass pebbles, and carefully rolled up the three scrolls one by one. After searching through the pile, he replaced them with a more detailed map of India, and two more overlays.

"You'll note here," he said, "that there are no large confluences, marked by larger X's as you saw on the other map. These wide rivers, as you call them, don't intersect, you see? However, there are several places where the smaller rivers overlap. And at those intersections, you'll see these very small red X's, representing weaker but still useful confluences—"

Here he removed the overlays, revealing the map beneath, and pointed to a smattering of tiny red X's.

"This cave, and it's associated Selectivam Ostium, is here," he said, pointing to one of the X's, "precisely where this X is marked."

"And so, this cave," I started.

"—Is accessible only through the use of a confluence. That's correct," finished the professor.

"You mean, that door is powered by the confluence? I thought it was supposed to be tables?" Olivia asked.

"Well, it is a rather small confluence," quipped the professor.

Olivia only raised her eyebrows.

"A table is more complicated, and operates rather differently. Plus, who is to say that those who enchanted the door knew anything about the tables at that time? And with the amount of power we have access to from this confluence —enough only to transport a few people a short distance—a door makes a lot more sense anyway."

"How?" she insisted.

"Consider how many people might you seat at a large table. Dozens, perhaps, maybe even more. But how many people may pass through a reasonably sized doorway at once? And over great distances, standing leads to other problems. With the knowledge I have and you have, that's really the best I can do for you at the moment. Suffice it to say for now that in the case of short travel through a weak confluence, it's more often—but not always—doors."

I'll remind the reader that although many magicians may have read about confluences in my first book, this entire history occurred years before this or my first book were published. Olivia and I knew of the confluences because of our history with the abductions, but they were not at the time widely understood nor accepted as fact. This revelation of the extent of their known realities was astounding, even to us.

Seeing that we had no immediate questions, the professor spoke again.

"This room currently holds four living people who know what a confluence is, and have used one to travel around the globe. An excessively rare group, and the largest such group to be gathered together in ages, I'm sure. It also holds the only four people who have ever seen these maps, or even know of their existence."

He began rolling them up as he continued.

"We will undoubtedly come back to these, as they are at the core of one of my life's works, which I want you to know more about. I've given you the charm to enter this room—

with practice, you could learn to use it. I plan on giving you much more before we're through, about confluences and other things. For now, realize and appreciate how much I trust you, and let's leave it at that."

Here he looked at Karthika. Appeal, I think, was in his eyes. After a pause, he continued.

"And that, I believe, answers the questions about why we're here, why it's such a great and safe place to meet, how the door works, et cetera. I know it is wildly insufficient for your curious natures, but it's all we really have time for now. Let's move forward, shall we? The earth is still spinning around the sun, even if we can't see it happening from here."

My own mind was ablaze with new dilemmas, most of them dim and covered in a mist of half-conceived infancy. I was unable to object, though I would have liked to sit and ponder for an hour on what had just happened. Spindlebrock finished rounding up the scrolls, and handed them back to Karthika, who went to replace them wherever it was they were held safe.

"Just in time, too. Lewis should be online by now. Follow me."

Chapter 13

A Viable Theory

The preceding chapters are, like all that I write, imperfect and only as close to the actual events and dialogue as I can recall. I must confess, reader, that it felt a little excessive by my standards, to spend so much energy explaining and reviewing such a brief segment of time; indeed, I could have simply said that we left the Cascabela and traveled to a safe house, where we gained new magical insights. That would have covered it. But you're aware, no doubt, of the importance of the confluences in what I have shared with you so far in my previous book; and I'm sure you can already comprehend that they play a part in what I share with you now. As you'll hopefully have an active interest (or at least a curiosity) in Spindlebrock's character and the progress that Olivia was making in her magical development—I figured the recollections would be worth your time and mine.

As for the meeting with Lewis, though I enjoy recalling my interactions with him as much as those of any of my friends, I'll spare the reader details and dialogue in favor of a (hopefully) more succinct summary.

After the rock slid closed behind Karthika, the rest of us made our way to the computers. Lewis was brought up on the large screen, and by and by he assisted us in reviewing elements of the security footage (another novel could be written on his technical experience, exploits, and skills—as I am not technologically inclined myself, I'll avoid embarrassing myself by attempting to describe them here), employee records, and schedules of Tamanna and the person she replaced, who was listed as Gwyenn Brennan on her file. There was no employee photo—at least not in the main records. Lewis searched through the system backups and found one that had been removed. It was indeed that same elusive Evalyn I had encountered at Bardo's in Adana.

Spindlebrock was more convinced than ever that we had found our suspect, and that Crane must be involved; that Evalyn was remotely connected to the crime scene, and that her employee records were altered, were proof enough for him. We hoped that by looking more closely at the security videos, we could catch her tampering with the scroll or display. We watched all the footage we could find of Evalyn on duty in the inner vault, going back several weeks before the theft.

Combing through the videos consumed tedious hours. We found nothing incriminating, and all but myself began to flag. Spindlebrock eventually postulated that Evalyn was perhaps just another one of the many of the casino's employees with a checkered past, trying to make a living however they could—though this couldn't explain the need for altering the employee record. Even so, he said, she was out of the equation a week before the scroll was first known to have disappeared; if she had opened it before she left, could the scroll case really have remained unsealed for so long without anyone noticing?

As I stubbornly and meticulously scanned and re-scanned the recordings, the others slowly turned to other interests; Spindlebrock began searching through the book on Magical Objects for the cloak that Olivia had seen Crane wearing, while Olivia and Karthika retired to a corner to talk about subjects I could imagine but not know. There was one video of Evalyn finishing a shift at the inner vault that was of particular interest to me, and which I reviewed carefully. Something in her general mannerisms was different, though I couldn't quite determine what it was. Her movements seemed more deliberate, her demeanor less open. And yet her actions didn't look, on the surface, to be of any consequence at all.

At length, after watching this last bit several times over, I had Lewis show me her movements after she left the vault that day. This was about a week prior to the theft, and the third to last time that she was on duty in the vaults before being replaced. Lewis had her employee file and work schedule pulled up on the screen as we watched, and we noted that according to her schedule she should have been on duty patrolling near the pools that afternoon; but as we watched, she did not exit the building at the back. Instead, she had a brief conversation with another guard, and she started an indoor sweep.

My curiosity was piqued. I watched the footage of Evalyn making her rounds in other parts of the building. It was clear from the video that she was avoiding people, and not making much effort in the execution of her duties. But the thing that struck me the most was her visit to a particular upper corridor, and a most meticulous check of a certain door and passageway in that corridor. It was the air conditioning service room, which I had visited myself almost as soon as I had arrived at the Cascabela.

I called Spindlebrock over to review the whole thing with me one more time, from the inner vault all the way up to the service room. As we watched, Olivia and Karthika joined us out of curiosity. The professor agreed that it was an interesting coincidence, but that all the guards checked the service room as part of their rounds on that route; and besides, there was no footage of Evalyn taking the scroll or even approaching the scroll case during her inner vault duties. There was, as I have pointed out previously, no video feed inside the service area itself.

We were all getting tired, and the clocks by now read close to ten in the evening. I think I hoped to discover more than I could actually see, and I believe I felt the impression of premonition—that thing called a "funny feeling"—but I could not convey or impress that on anyone else in the party. Spindlebrock asked Karthika to procure something for us all to eat, and while she sat with us watching the videos, plates and food floated over our heads from a small cabinet and began arranging themselves on the table. I addressed Karthika.

"You slide the stone that blocks the entrance to this cave. Do you think you could lift it?"

"I could, but it's much easier to slide it."

"Yes, but you could lift it if you wanted to. How high, and for how long?"

"Well, dear, it depends on how I'm feeling. Magic takes energy, as you surely know. On a good day, I could probably lift it for several minutes, practically as high as I liked."

I glanced from Spindlebrock to her, and back. He shrugged.

"So?"

"Don't you see? Telekinesis could have been used to lift the heavy brass top off your scroll display!"

"Well, I suppose—but that doesn't answer any of our other questions. To lift the lid off my display would be rude, indeed, but it's not a burglary. We need to know how the rest was accomplished, that's what is important in my mind."

I waited for more, but he had nothing more to say. He looked at me, confused.

"You mean," I continued slowly, "that you really don't see how this might matter?"

He shrugged again and sat back in his seat.

"Well then, let's go and eat; and if you're willing, Karthika, I'll ask you to assist me with something afterward if you would, please."

After wrapping things up with Lewis for the evening, we all sat to have a bite to eat. Everyone seemed relieved to move on from our work without another thought; even so, Spindlebrock kept a casual eye on me as I scrawled in my notebook. I confess that I was feeling quite self-satisfied concerning the track that my mind had caught. I looked forward anxiously to the end of the meal, when I would have my final exhibition on the subject.

As we finished, I queried Karthika casually.

"Regarding your library, I recall you bringing up several tall file cabinets—I think the book the professor has been searching through came from one of them, is that right?"

"Yes."

"In point of fact, I noticed that when you cast the enchantment to bring that cabinet up, you produced a small key to unlock it, before retrieving the book. Why is that?"

"Why is what?"

"Why would you keep such a cabinet locked, when it is already protected by a fantastic and rare charm?"

She puzzled for a few moments.

"I don't know, now that you mention it. Out of habit, I suppose. It's quite amusing, really. The thing is, I had that cabinet for a long time before I learned to enchant it that way. I think in my mind, it's somehow proper to lock it."

"That makes sense," I agreed. "I have another curiosity about that cabinet. Would it be inappropriate for me to ask to see it once more? Could we all look?"

"Certainly, that wouldn't be a problem at all. Cyrus, have you had a chance to look through that book?"

"Adequately," he replied. "I'm quite finished with it, actually. We can take this opportunity to return it."

We all got up and made our way to the rocks, where Karthika called up the cabinet. She produced her key and was about to open it, when I interrupted her.

"Wait, please. May I?"

She handed me the key, which I examined carefully.

"You see these little peaks and valleys?" I asked her.

"Well, they're like many keys. The most common variety I would say."

"Yes, very common. And do you know how they work?"

She shook her head.

"Inside the lock, there are what are known as tumblers. Small pins, cut at different lengths, moving inside cylinders. When you insert the correct key, the cylinders rest in these valleys, aligning the different length ends to allow the lock to rotate open. Have you seen any kind of diagram or cross-section of this?"

"No, it's not something that I'm terribly interested in, dear."

I took out my notebook, and flipped it open to a sketch of a tumbler lock that I had worked on while we ate. She examined it carefully, and I explained the different elements of the diagram.

"Why do you use this key to open this cabinet?" I asked at length.

"It is the key that matches the lock."

"Yes, but why use a key at all?"

She looked at me, confused.

"You can move plates around a room without looking. You can lift or slide incredibly heavy things. I must assume you could move incredibly small and light things if you wished, is that a correct assumption?"

Spindlebrock cleared his throat and stepped closer, but said nothing.

"Certainly, with ease."

"And, you don't have to see what you're moving, just to be entirely clear."

"That's true, as long as I'm within a certain distance and can visualize it."

"And so I ask again: Why use this key? With the talent and ability you have, couldn't you manipulate the tumblers, and open the cabinet without it?"

She laughed.

"Well, I suppose so. But I'd have to have studied the mechanism first, I guess, and then I'd have to memorize the pattern for each of the locks in my library—"

Here she motioned to the quantity of rocks.

"To do it quickly, you'd need to memorize the key patterns, but that wouldn't be necessary if you were going to move each tumbler—trial and error—until the cylinder engaged. You could do that by understanding the basics of the mechanism," I replied. "You do believe you could at least manipulate the tumblers, with this diagram I showed you, don't you?"

"Yes, I suppose I could."

"Can we try?"

She agreed to give it a go. We reviewed the diagram again. She spent several minutes looking intently at the lock, apparently reaching out with her gift and feeling how it all fit together. I inquired as to how long such an investigation might take with no prior knowledge of the mechanism; she replied that with no knowledge at all, it might take hours, but with the diagram and explanation, she could feel what was going on within minutes.

Finally, she made the attempt. I've seen many locks picked in my time, and have even picked some myself, but I've never seen anything like a lock evidently picking itself. The mechanism shook and rattled, sometimes enough to jostle the whole cabinet. After what felt like forever, the lock finally sprung open.

"I did it! Cyrus, look at that!"

He smiled, but didn't quite look satisfied. I hurried to continue.

"Very good Karthika! Now, the first time you pick a lock, it's a messy affair. An amateur might even ruin a lock when using metal tools, though I don't think that's much of a risk in this case. Do you think you could do it again? This time, pay special attention to delicacy. I'd like to see if you can perform that same task, but without disrupting the lock or cabinet quite so much. Imagine that you're trying not to trigger a movement sensor. Give it your best effort, if you would."

She nodded, with a pleased and determined look on her face. I locked the cabinet, and she set to work again. Her focus was incredible, and with her previous success and experience to help her along, she did the work easily more than three times as fast, with very little movement of the mechanism and no movement of the cabinet.

"Perfect! You've done wonderfully, and on only your second attempt!"

I turned to Spindlebrock.

"Your thoughts about Telekinesis being an insufficient explanation—do you wish to revise them?"

He laughed.

"You have me, Thomas, you have me. I confess that I hadn't thought about using Telekinesis in this way. The scroll case is a tumbler-based system. We'd have to have Karthika examine it to be sure, but it's quite possible that she could do this same trick in that situation."

I beamed. It's not often that I think of something before the professor does, and it was a good feeling.

"But," he continued, "that's still only a portion of the story. The videos don't show her taking the scroll out. So, where was it? What's the rest of your theory?"

Karthika replaced the book and we made our way back to the sitting area as we talked.

"It all came to me at once, like floodgates opening, when Karthika was preparing our food. Everything was going right over our heads. Don't you see? If we hadn't looked up, we wouldn't have even noticed it."

"Yes! That's right! Thomas, you genius!"

"The camera pointed at the case is angled so you can't see the top; remember, we couldn't see where the glass met the brass. Gently lift the top—only the guard on duty would see it, the camera would be oblivious—then float the scroll right out. Of course, the harder part would be opening the scroll case in the first place. Evalyn would have had to study it for some time, as Karthika demonstrated—who knows how long in total, since she had no real knowledge of the mechanism, and since she would have to work so very gently, so as not to trigger the alarm."

"But she would have had ample time for that; all the time she needed, during her employment there."

"Exactly. This wasn't an impulse, it was planned, and she was prepared. I'm thinking she likely opened the scroll case first. Perhaps she even slid the scroll out before lifting the brass top—"

"If it were me," Karthika broke in, "that's how I'd do it. Open the scroll case, take out the scroll, then do the heavy lifting last."

"And, you could manage it all in that sequence, correct? Keeping the scroll aloft and lifting the top?" I asked.

"Of course! I can manage dozens of items at once."

"Good," I continued. "So we have things that far. Now, we all saw from the videos that she didn't drop the scroll into her own hands. I have two theories about what happened next. First, the cameras throughout most of the building are placed high—I noticed this when we first walked through. They are about a foot and a half from the ceiling. She could have floated the scroll at the ceiling level, and walked it out of the vaults."

Spindlebrock looked pensive.

"That seems rather risky," he said at length. "She would have had it out of view of the camera, certainly, but not out view of anyone who happened to look up. Plus, what would she do when she got out of the vaults? Much of the building has lower ceilings, and I'm certain some of those come into view of the cameras."

"Exactly what I thought," I replied. "There are several camera viewpoints that she passed through that show the ceiling, especially the hallway by the service access. We would have seen a curious floating scroll in the video, I'm certain."

"And so, what is your other theory?"

"The one that makes the most sense: Evalyn extracted the scroll, and floated it carefully to the vents at the top of the inner vault. She removed the vent cover and guided the scroll carefully into it. You said that there are vibration sensors in the duct work, do you know if those are installed

168

on the smaller ducts of the vaults, or only the larger ducts in the building?"

"Only the larger ones, those that might accommodate a petite and insane intruder."

"Right, and that makes perfect sense. Why put any kind of security on a vent that couldn't fit a person? So, into the ducts went the scroll. Evalyn guided it through, carefully, all the way to the service room."

"Karthika," interjected the professor, "does that sound at all plausible?"

"I think so. However, I would want to know if all of the ducts are visible?"

"Inside the vault, they are easy enough to see," I replied. "But in the main portion of the building, they are hidden."

"Then," she said, "she must have had some kind of a map or diagram of the construction, to do it reliably."

"Indeed," Spindlebrock muttered, as he began to pace.

"But it is possible, and it's the best theory we have so far, professor. If Evalyn could have gotten some of the building plans, she could have gotten the scroll through to that room. It's the only thing that makes any sense."

"It does make sense," he conceded, pausing in his pacing. "There's only one problem with it—if she could do all of that, why not retrieve the scroll right then, and walk out of the building with it? There are no cameras in that service area, she could have concealed the scroll on her person and left. Why leave it there, for her cohort to come back for later?"

"Yes, that does seem odd. Maybe she came back for it herself? Maybe she was the one in the video?"

"I can't account for it at all," he continued, still thinking. "It makes no logical sense, to leave something so valuable sitting in a room unprotected, and for an entire week—and no, it wasn't her who came back for it, I'm fairly certain of that. Their physical profiles are different. There wasn't much video of the burglar who retrieved the scroll, but enough to see a height and build difference."

He resumed his pacing.

"And," he continued, "there's another issue. This is all good and fine when we ask Karthika about what she can or can't do, but she is one of the best Telekenetics that I know. There are perhaps only a few in the entire world that could manage the weight and the delicacy and the distance. Delphine could do it, I think, and—"

He gasped and froze in place, a look of shock on his face. He looked so taken aback that we all three asked him what the matter was in chorus.

"Pieces," he whispered. His eyes darted back and forth, evidently racing with his mind to find some obscure thought. We waited for more, and after some time, he continued.

"It's all coming together. At least, I think it is. It's only theories at present, but it does open a window of opportunity, if what I think is happening, is happening. Thomas, answer me this—"

He waited, and I nodded for him to continue.

"You described to me once what it felt like when you grabbed Evalyn's hand, in Bardo's that time when she came to see you. Tell me again."

I recalled it vividly.

"It was a searing pain, it went up my arm. I pulled back immediately, then blacked out."

"Yes, that's right. I couldn't account for it. Your room, I think, was broken into on that day as well, was it not?"

"It was. Bardo was very alarmed."

"Interesting. It's pieces, that's all—possibilities but not proof. Still, if it turns out to be true, there may still be a chance to retrieve the scroll, but we have to hurry."

It was our turn now to gasp. Spindlebrock walked over to Karthika and embraced her, thanking her aloud and then whispering something in her ear.

"Come," he then said to Olivia and me. "We must go at once."

Chapter 14

Careworn in Kreva

After saying our goodbyes and thanking Karthika, we left the safety of the cave with its massive stone barrier and its charmed Selectivam Ostium, and were back on the road with Spindlebrock once again at the wheel. It was close to midnight, but not one of us was sleepy. Olivia broke the silence.

"The perfect time of day for hunting ghosts, I think. Where are we heading?"

Spindlebrock laughed. He sounded far more light-hearted than I felt.

"I know my scroll hunt has become consuming, but don't worry, I haven't forgotten the ghost. Before we go back to Toronto, we will revisit the Cascabela, and we'll see how far the three of us can get working together on that problem."

Olivia smiled at him.

"But you haven't really answered me: Where are we going now?"

Spindlebrock swerved to avoid an errant farm animal in the middle of the road.

"It comes down to this," he explained. "Someone was hired to steal the scroll."

"What do you mean?" I asked.

"Just that the people who stole the scroll didn't steal it for themselves. The thieves weren't the ones who wanted it. They were hired to do the job."

"And how could you know that?"

"I have two supporting hypotheses. First, I suggest that the vast majority of those who might be interested in having the scroll, simply wouldn't have the necessary skill to steal it. That's not to say that a person with the particular skill of high-end magical burglary couldn't be interested for themselves—the scroll is of sufficient value to be a target for anyone—but it's almost too much of a target. It's too well known, stealing it would bring out the most skilled magicians and put them on your trail forever.

"Second, we have some very shocking discrepancies in the case. The one that stood out to me the most, after you craftily revealed a most probable method, means, time, and suspect—"

He nodded toward me, then continued.

"—was that the burglars didn't simply take the scroll out of the building. Why the theatrics? Why stage a cunning removal from the vault, only to delay getting the stolen property off the premises quickly and safely?"

He paused as if waiting for an answer, but none came.

"To this question I could only postulate that for some reason, the pair valued something else above obtaining the scroll. They must have believed without a doubt that they would get it, seen that as a foregone conclusion—which means they had inside help."

"I thought Evalyn was the inside help?" chimed in Olivia.

"I'm not so sure—in fact, everything points to Evalyn working as one of the hired burglars."

"But she works for Crane!" I added.

"Perhaps. We believe that she did work for Crane at one point, but that doesn't mean she still does. And, as she escaped us after Turkey and was never interrogated, we don't know the nature of her relationship with him. We assume that it was the same as all the others, but we don't know that."

"True, but—"

"No buts, Thomas. Assumptions may be fine starting points for theories, but they don't hold value until proven, and shouldn't arrest other theories in their development! What we know in this case is that Evalyn worked with another burglar to steal the scroll, but didn't take it off the property herself. The two were hired—whether by Crane or someone else, we don't know—but they weren't controlled by whoever hired them. They were allowed their own methods.

"These were experts; they would have to be among the foremost expert magical burglars in the world to attempt such a heist. No one would tell them how to do their job. And, as experts, they would know that with the value of the target object, the world's foremost forensic magician would be called in to investigate. And, of course, they knew that I would be involved as well."

I smiled in the dark at his compliment. As to his opinion of my skill and position in the magical commonality, I wasn't as convinced.

"So," he continued, "given the probability that someone with interest in the scroll wouldn't have the skill to steal it themselves, and given the odd methods employed in the burglary, I believe that it was a commissioned job."

"I still don't get it," I said. "All of it makes sense, except the theatrics, as you call them. How do those indicate it was a hired job?"

"Because the only way to account for this delay in removing the scroll, is that they were trying to send a message."

"A message? To whom?"

"To us, the two magicians that they knew would be called in to investigate."

Whether from the late hour, the recently more curved country roads, or the case itself, the wheels in my head were grinding to a halt. The professor seemed to notice, but continued without pause.

"Experts with skill and experience aren't likely to make nonsensical mistakes. Therefore, we must assume their method was purposeful. As it didn't help them obtain their end more quickly or efficiently, we must assume subterfuge."

"Now you're doing all the assuming," I quipped.

"But not to impede possibilities and close doors, Thomas, that's an important distinction. Always use assumption to your advantage and never let it hinder you—but this is not a classroom! Do you agree or not, that their behavior seemed engineered to send us, the investigators, a message?"

"Yes, I think you might be right. But why? If you're hired to do a job, why bother with subterfuge?"

"Because whoever hired them, hired the wrong people and didn't manage them properly. Burglars are, above all else, interested in themselves. They had their target, and probably had some additional help, resources, and initial payment. They knew they could get the scroll. But why stop at what they were first offered? If someone was willing to pay for the scroll to be stolen, perhaps someone else would be willing to pay even more to have it for themselves? Brevig is wealthy, and that isn't much of a secret. There are many others who are wealthy and who might be interested. Perhaps, given the chance, another buyer would outdo the initial contract."

"You mean, you think the burglars were sending a signal somehow, that they'd be willing to negotiate?"

"I think," replied the professor, "that we have approximately twelve hours to find out."

* * *

It would be ludicrous to report that in a few short hours we visited Hyderabad in Telangana, a remote village in Odisha, then Bangladesh and Nepal, and ended up in Belarus. I should say, it would be ludicrous if you weren't already aware of the professor's extensive knowledge of the confluences.

There are no confluences in southern India that can be used for long distance travel, and so after driving to the airport in Salem (where we left our luggage in the car, Spindlebrock assuring us that we wouldn't need it), we continued our travel with a short flight to Hyderabad. In the famous Salar Jung Museum, where Spindlebrock seemed to have immediate and unlimited access, there is an interesting selection of tables, preserved as exhibits—literally anyone can see them. Their real purpose you can guess—we used one to travel a short distance to a small and ancient estate in Odisha, and onward in the same manner until we connected with the more powerful confluence in Nepal that let us travel all the way to Belarus in an instant.

It is perhaps amazing to you, reader, that Spindlebrock would travel this way with us, thus revealing to both Olivia and me traveling spells that he likely had never revealed to another living being. It was certainly amazing to me at the time, and had it not been for his remarks in the cave with Karthika, I'm not sure if I would have understood it at all. I believe Olivia shared my wonder, and wished as I did that we could spend more time delving into what exactly we were learning; but time seemed not to be on our side.

In the intervals of these twilight travels Spindlebrock explained that the magical criminal underworld had many outlets for stolen goods, but only one that was considered worthy of the most magnificently costly wares: the Glebovich Auction House, in Kreva, Belarus. The scroll, if it were to be offered for sale anywhere, would be offered there, at their annual auction.

The morning sun was straining its way through a grimy, half-boarded window when we arrived in Kreva. With each progression in our journey Spindlebrock had grown more and more withdrawn; he was now entirely silent as he motioned for us to follow him out of the dilapidated house that was our final landing place. The countryside was pleasant enough in the morning light and mist, but an anxious sense of anticipation clouded my mind. We walked down a gravel path and met with a paved road, which we followed toward the sparse township. I was impressed by two interesting and safe looking churches, whose steeples beckoned from afar—but alas, we stopped at a far less inviting little dwelling on the edge of the village, long before we got anywhere near them.

As we knocked, something informed me that this was a kind of an inn, though no sign marked it as such. We were greeted by an ancient and bowed hostess, who gruffly welcomed us in a dialect which I later learned was called Trasianka, a mixture of Belarusian and Russian. After we entered and Spindlebrock made our wishes known (I assume), she waved a crooked finger at a young man planted in front of a television screen glowing with some video game. The controller flew from his hands at her enchantment, and he uttered a groan and protest that were also in Transianka, though they seemed to me to be in a universally understood tone. In spite of his attitude he was prompt about getting up to help, and his protest turned to excitement when he realized we were speaking English among ourselves. As he led us to our room, he struck up a conversation.

"Wow, man! Most of our visitors are from Minsk and Moscow all the time, you know? We get a lot from Europe too, like mostly from eastern—Türkiye, and Georgia, Romania. We got a guy from Spain here today too, and from Australia!"

He laughed, at some unshared memory it seemed to me.

"So where do you guys come from," he continued. "America?"

He was looking at me, so I answered.

"I'm American, yes, but we all live in Canada."

"Cool! So what is it like in America, huh? You get to go to the beaches and burger joints all the time, no? It's good stuff my brother, I wish I was there!"

It was my turn to laugh. He was friendly, and continued in small talk while he fluffed our pillows, straightened things out, and generally took more time that was needed to get us situated. As he spoke, a lanky ginger tabby cat snuck into the room and started snaking itself in a figure eight around his feet.

"Penny, shoo! It's my cat, she's named for an American coin. Go, Penny! See, her fur is like the color of copper!"

Stooping down and scooping up the purring cat, he glanced at Spindlebrock then whispered to us all in a more serious tone.

"I know why you're all here, you know. We only get to have this many people at rare times, when rare items are for sale, if you catch my meanings. Good luck. You will need it, eh? My name is Sergei."

He held out his hand, which I took. His grip was firm, and he looked me in the eyes as I gave him my name. This was repeated with Olivia, and then Spindlebrock—but when he heard the professor's name, his face dropped and his hand froze mid-shake. His mouth opened and closed, guppy-like, but no words came. The professor just looked at him, his face devoid of all emotion. The young man dropped his hand when Penny started licking it. In a serious tone, he addressed the professor in his native Transianka and they had a brief conversation. After he was gone, and as we were setting in, Spindlebrock explained their interview.

"It was nothing that I didn't expect. He asked me if Glebovich knew I was here; I answered that I doubted it greatly. He pressed me to know for certain, and I told him that while nothing would shock me more, I had no doubt that he would know it within the hour. This he at first took as an insult, an insinuation that he would be reporting me; until he realized I was talking about the old woman and not him. He assured me that if I needed anything, I could ask him—he was a nice young man, actually."

"Glebovich is the one who runs the auction house, I guess?" I asked as I plopped onto a small but cozy high-backed reading chair.

"Indeed. It has been in his family's control for generations. I thought I mentioned that."

He hadn't, but I didn't argue the point. He continued.

"Our hostess is well known to me, as is Glebovich. And I hardly know which one hates me more."

"What should that have to do with anything?" asked Olivia. She was relaxing on a couch.

"We'll see. What I do know is that she will be in contact with him as soon as she feels she can do so without detection. I don't care, and so I won't bother to watch her, of course. The auction starts in a few hours, I suggest we get a little sleep."

He did care. In fact, for the first time on this trip he looked truly careworn.

In addition to the furniture Olivia and I occupied, the room had two rickety twin beds. Spindlebrock, who would have normally deferred, fell into one and buried his head in the pillow. I glanced at Olivia with raised eyebrows, and motioned for her to take the other bed. She shook her head and leaned back, closing her eyes. Examining the old bed, I decided that the chair was probably the better option, and before long we were all sleeping quietly.

Chapter 15

Den Mechty

Olivia was shaking me by the shoulder gently. As I opened my eyes and saw her standing over me, I thought almost immediately of my toothbrush, currently sitting in my luggage in an airport parking lot in the middle of India. Apparently she understood exactly where my thinking would be—she was holding out a small plastic bag.

"There's a market down the street. Spindlebrock bought us a few things—there's a toothbrush in there, bathroom is down the hall on the left. I think everyone else has left already, Spindlebrock went to talk to our hosts about something."

I thanked her, made my way to the bathroom, and cleaned myself up as best I could. When I returned, Spindlebrock was back, a few garment bags slung over one arm.

"There you are, good morning. I was just explaining to Olivia that the Glebovich Auction House has a very specific dress code for this particular event. Look."

He set the garment bags on a bed and unzipped the top bag, revealing a traditional white linen shirt with fascinating red embroidery, gray wool pants, and a bright red embroidered belt. This outfit was mine. Spindlebrock's outfit more or less matched, and Olivia's was a dress in similar material, with a black-and-red vest. Each outfit had a head covering—a hat for the professor and me, and a sort of wrap for Olivia.

"And why do we have to wear these?" was Olivia's response.

"To fit in. These are traditional clothing items, and today is the Kreva Day of Dreams—Den Mechty. It's an annual magical holiday and auction, dating back some generations. The magicians in Kreva cast a spell on the non-magical townsfolk, putting them all to sleep. They dream of living that day out, going about their lives in a sort of rose-colored light; a rest from their actual labors. When they awake, they don't know that they've missed a day, the dream is that real. This is why we saw no one while we were walking here this morning.

"In the afternoon, the magicians gather in Kreva castle, where the Glebovich family casts a spell which allows all those present to re-live a former time of cultural prosperity. The spell only affects the area inside the castle walls, and it lasts for a few hours. During that time, Glebovich runs his auction. Long ago it used to be a real celebration, but now it is only a venue for wealthy magicians who wish to buy and sell relics, potions, and items that are considered too valuable—or too dangerous—for the general magical public."

He handed me my outfit, and instructed me to change in the bathroom, which I did. As I was coming back down the hall, I overheard Olivia and the Professor talking. I paused at the door to listen.

"I've never done it before. It sounds dangerous, what if —"

"It's no danger that I'm not willing to risk, let that be on me. This must be tried. I'm not asking you to succeed, I'm only asking you to try. Please."

She hesitated, and I walked in.

"Try what?"

They both looked at me blankly for a few moments.

"There's something you both need to understand about this event," the professor began at length. "It will feel familiar to each of you, but to each of you in a different way. Thomas, do you recall in Turkey, the old hotel that we visited?"

"The Mazi?"

"No, the very old hotel, the one in ruins."

"Oh, yes! How could I forget that?"

"This will be like that, for you, except you won't be confined to a table—the effect will be on the whole castle. For you, Olivia, it will be something else I think, if we have an arrangement."

He didn't wait for an answer.

"The plan is simple. Olivia will take this Signum Dominii—the sign of ownership."

He removed a large coin from his pocket and handed it to her.

"It is a magical token, one that proves that you represent a magician with sufficient funds to participate in the auction and make good on any bids. As neither of you possesses a fortune of repute, this will serve both to grant you entry, and to allow you to bid on the scroll, if it appears."

"How does it work? Couldn't someone forge one of these?" she asked.

"They could perhaps forge the coin, but there is a spell. This object is inscribed with runes that represent the name Lucas Brevig, who formed this coin and performed the signature spell while it was still molten metal. At the door of the castle they will read the name, and attempt a counter-spell. Should there be any deception in how you obtained this token—meaning that you don't actually represent Lucas Brevig and his interests—then the counter-spell would succeed, and you would be discovered.

"I won't be going with you," he continued. "You'll be entering alone. An object as valuable and rare as the scroll will likely be last on the docket, so you'll have time to observe and understand the proceedings. In essence, when it is time to bid, you'll do so by holding up the token. Olivia, you will have to do the bidding, as the token is now tied to you. Give the token to no one else, or the Signum Dominii will be broken, do you understand?"

She eyed the coin intently, weighing it in her open palm.

"And you think this will work? I still think it sounds too dangerous."

I took these statements to be connected with those which I had overheard in the hall, though I later learned they were not.

"It will work, and if it does not, I alone bear the blame."

For me, the anxiety that had been building up was pushed to overflowing when Spindlebrock revealed that he would not accompany us.

"Why aren't you coming? We don't even speak the language—there's too much at stake! Why don't you just come?" I implored.

"Don't worry about the language, this event is attended by people from all over the globe, and English is the agreed language. As for me coming, I cannot, as I am forbidden.

Glebovich barred me from his auctions many years ago, and I've never attempted to attend one since. He's not a magician that any sane person would intentionally misuse—yes, I see your eyes getting big, Thomas. Even I fear some magicians. I am not alone at the top."

After he said this, he laughed heartily.

"I'm sorry, but your eyes went from alarmed to piqued in an instant. Yes, I'm arrogant, I know that and I apologize to you both. I don't generally care what people think of me, but your opinions matter a great deal to my heart; one day, you'll better understand my pomp.

"Now, given the goods Glebovich needs to move, I half think he would actually let me in today—but I feel that it's better this way. I'm hardly a favorite among the kind of crowd that he'll have anyway. There are the big eyes again! You two have nothing to worry about from the crowd or Glebovich, he won't transfer his feelings toward me onto you. He's far too pragmatic for that. If anything, he'll take it as a high compliment that I didn't dare show my face. You'll be perfectly safe. Even the criminals agree to behave in this setting."

"So if you're not coming with us, then why do you have a costume?"

"I could hardly blend in anywhere in town today without one, Thomas. I'll follow after the gates are closed, and stand outside, eagerly awaiting the results of your efforts."

Chapter 16

The Auction

The gates loomed before us. A procession of magicians had been streaming in through them all morning, and Olivia and I were toward the tail end of the line. As our turn approached, she whispered in my ear.

"I haven't seen anyone else use one of these tokens yet, Thomas. I don't know what to do with it!"

When our moment came, she simply held up the token (rather too close to the guard's face) without saying a word. The guard peeked around the coin at us, then shouted a few brusque commands to another sentinel who rushed to obey by disappearing through the gate. Presently he rejoined us, followed by a tottering old man dressed in a flowing black cloak. He spoke a perfect, if drawling, British English.

"You'll have to excuse the guards. We get so few Sig-num Do-mi-nii anymore—you are only the second today—and the guards don't read runes, much less command the counter spell. Now, let's see."

Without touching it, he leaned forward to inspect the coin, mouthing the runes and then translating the sounds aloud.

"Lu-cas Bre-vig," he said haltingly.

He seemed pleased with his efforts for a brief moment, before an understanding of the name he had just uttered settled on him.

"Lucas Brevig? You two young magicians propose to represent Lucas Brevig?"

He was indignant. Without another word, he produced his wand, aimed it at the coin and uttered a spell. As he finished, a visible double halo formed around the coin for several seconds.

The old man watched, then cast a furtive and searching glance around the remaining crowd.

"Remarkable. Absolutely remarkable. Well, your passport is valid, as absurd as that seems to me."

He signaled the guards, who asked us to sign our names in a large book. When we were told to enter, the old man had already gone.

The scene inside the castle was underwhelming. Though the front wall and gate had been restored, most of the castle was still in ruins. By that I mean that much of the outer wall and two ancient towers were piles of rubble, decimated by war, weather, time, and neglect. What was left of the structure enclosed a large, square field of grass, devoid of anything apart from the many small groups of magicians loitering about.

Olivia and I stepped off to the side and stood near the gate wall, watching silently. The steady trickle of newcomers soon slowed, and eventually died out. As the crowd became aware of the fact that no one else was being admitted, they quieted, and slowly parted to form a path leading from the gate into the middle of the field.

All at once, with a jumble of dance, music, and song, the gate burst open. Two groups of dancers, male and female, led the charge, working the crowd into an ever larger circle to give them room as they snaked and spun before us. Separated at first, the men and women eventually met and joined one another in the middle of the path, dancing their way further into what I believe is called the bailey. The band that followed was boisterously loud, heard long before they were seen. They carried traditional instruments of every sort, which I'm completely unqualified to describe; only I will say that they had string and wind and percussion, all playing a rousing traditional Belarusian tune.

An array of guards wearing quasi-military outfits followed in ranks, marching in lockstep. They were in six rows, broken in the middle by an additional row of the largest, fittest guards, all dressed in bright red tunics. In the center of this row of red was a massive specimen of a man, barrel-chested and towering, with a thick grizzled beard that would have added a foot to his height had it been atop his bald head.

As soon as he came into view, waving and smiling and shouting something in his mother tongue, the crowd erupted with cheers.

"That must be Glebovich."

I leaned in and spoke loudly so Olivia could hear, but she didn't need to validate my supposition, as the crowd immediately began chanting his name. They carried on as he made his way into the center of the bailey. He seemed to know exactly where he was going, to the very step, and when he arrived he turned and raised his arms, a wand in each hand.

The crowd cheered one last time, but quickly quieted. In a flurry of movement that seemed far too coordinated (almost disturbingly so) for such a mass of humans, they began arranging themselves in tidy rows before him, and in short order they were marshaled like a small army, in two bodies on the right and left, with an aisle in the center.

Olivia and I looked at one another, dumbfounded.

"Friends!" shouted Glebovich, "We have waited one full year for this day of celebration, of the glory of Kreva restored, and the auction—"

He visibly faltered, his wands lowering slightly. When he started again, his voice was weighted with the struggle of stoicism over emotion.

"—the auction that my great and powerful ancestors inaugurated, which has sustained and dignified this, our esteemed land of magical tradition, for these many years.

"This year," he continued, "will be like no other, for we will see rarities that we have not seen return to this auction since the very beginning, the first Den Mechty. It is not for me to reveal what valuable objects await your consideration, my friends—but I think many of you have been told that this would be an auction not to be missed. And so, let it begin!"

What followed his brief speech was the most elaborate display of wand work that I have ever witnessed. His whole body moved in a rhythmic motion that can only be described as a dance, as the words—some sung, some spoken, others shouted, and still others in whispers that none could hear but the speaker himself—wove themselves into the very air we breathed. The effect was intoxicating, and as he achieved the feat whose secrets still live and die within his family alone, the world around us vibrated and blurred and swirled with color. I felt a rush of wind; was dizzy, but not afraid.

Olivia grabbed my hand, and focus returned to a degree. I watched in amazement as a vision of the castle in what must have been its full glory, grew and superimposed itself on what I knew to be real and present. The two towers raised themselves from the dust, their open windows adorned with garland of living yet gossamer green. The walls repaired themselves, it seemed to me, from rubble to robustness, straight and stable and strong. And before us both—our vantage point near the gate placed the scene squarely in front of us—the traditional buildings of the bailey appeared, a castle's interior village, where there was nothing but grass just moments prior.

It's difficult to bend words to the task of instilling the feelings that I experienced as this spell was performed, but as it was completed, the scene—and the sentiments that it imparted—were perhaps a little simpler to describe. It felt, as Spindlebrock had predicted, much like it felt when I was sitting in the ruins of that hotel in Turkey, in some part of the confluence in that region that is now known to my readers and others. In that past case, Spindlebrock had used a much simpler spell (it seemed to me), which involved an enchanted table. In this case, a like effect was accomplished on a much larger scale, and without any apparent physical accessory. Or, perhaps the entire castle was the enchanted object, taking the place of the table.

It wasn't until this transformation was complete that Olivia loosened her grip on my hand. We stared in amazement at the large building before us, a hall which now housed the auction-goers. Large double doors stood wide open, readily revealing a cavernous but well-lit interior. The attendees had arranged themselves almost perfectly so as to be able to sit in seats that were already there after the charm was complete, and that is how they now appeared. The auction had already started, with Glebovich seated on a small balustrade with his guards, and an auctioneer leading the proceedings.

"Fascinating! Could this be part of a confluence?"

I thought out loud as we watched from a distance, the first item coming out for auction. It was a magical relic, a sort of staff (which have been more common to some locations throughout history, used by magicians in place of wands) from northern Africa.

"I was thinking maybe this was some kind of illusion," Olivia answered. "I thought confluences were used to travel to other locations, like the way we got to Kreva. Why do you think this could be a confluence?"

"It's true that they're used to travel, but Spindlebrock showed me something once. He said it was a confluence, but it was more like this experience than the traveling that we've been through to get here. We sat at a table in a broken down old hotel, and he had a sort of complex charm—it felt similar to what Glebovich was doing, until you took my hand—and we saw the hotel the way it was in its prime. Not only the hotel, we saw the people, the way they were dressed, the way the room was setup; everything, just as if the hotel wasn't in ruins, but a running, working hotel. He absolutely prohibited me from getting up from the table until the charm was countered and we were back in the ruins."

"So, he used a confluence to do what exactly? Did he explain it to you?"

"He never did. But, I had a theory. The people, the way they were dressed, the hotel looking new and active; everything looked like it was from a particular time period. I thought that perhaps he had found a way to travel in time. It sounds crazy, but it's the best I could think of."

"But, you didn't actually go anywhere? You said he didn't let you get up from the table."

"That's right, we only looked. He was so insistent—protective almost, the way he kept telling me to stay in my seat—that I thought there must have been some danger in us getting up."

Olivia pondered silently for a few moments as we watched the auction continue. The African staff had sold for a handsome sum, and a small but ornate feathered wizard's cap was now on the block.

"You couldn't get up from the table in that hotel," she said at length. "Yet there's a whole group of people here, just sitting in that old building on chairs that weren't here a few minutes ago, having an auction like it's no big deal. And no table in sight."

"Yeah," I whispered, as people in the back row were starting to turn and look at us through the wide doorway.

"Did you say you saw people? In the hotel, last time with Spindlebrock I mean," she too had lowered her voice.

"Yes, I recall it well. I could even hear their voices a little."

"But there are no people here that I can see, apart from those who entered with us."

"Perhaps we've traveled to a time when they were all somewhere else? Maybe on purpose—of course! Couldn't this be Den Mechty, the day of dreams, but in the past? Everyone would be asleep! His spell, if similar to Spindlebrock's spell in the hotel, could have brought us here to this time in particular, on purpose."

"It's a good theory. I guess I can't think of a better one, anyway."

She looked around.

"But, I do wish there were some people here. To sit on a chair or look at buildings that have long since fallen into ruin is one thing, but people are the real mystery to me."

"That reminds me," I ventured. "Spindlebrock told me that I'd have a similar experience to the one in the hotel, but he said you would have a different sort of experience. What did he mean by that?"

"I don't know yet. I think I have an idea, kind of. It felt like something that happened to me in India. Something to do with what I learned there. Sanjay also asked me not to move from the spot I was in that time, like Spindlebrock did with you getting up from that table. I don't know, we'll see."

She didn't offer anything more, and so we both turned our attention to the auction. Olivia didn't seem to want to enter the building, so we continued to watch from outside the doors. Though the magical items were amazing—and their selling costs just as awe-inspiring—I couldn't help but feel a rising sense of anxiety about the possibility of the scroll appearing on the auction block. The auctioneer was announcing items in the format, "Lot nine out of thirty-five", and so the proceedings had the feel of a countdown. When he got to lot number thirty-three, Olivia, who had also seemed increasingly anxious and agitated, suddenly turned toward the castle gate.

I watched as she removed the Signum Dominii token from her pocket, and placed it on the ground in front of her. She glanced at me briefly.

"Keep a lookout, there's something I have to try."

I did as she said. The auction and all those concerned with it were in the building, and all were engrossed in the ever-more-interesting items on the block. From the corner of my eye, I watched her. She closed her eyes, and started into a spell in some ancient and unknown language. This continued for a time, but the effects were unseen to me. The spell was repeated, with more fervor, but still with no apparent effect. Finally, she opened her eyes.

"It's not working."

I turned to her, and saw that she was distressed. Instinctively wanting to be helpful, and forgetting that Spindlebrock had asked to not let anyone else touch it, I stooped down to retrieve the token for her. As I stood, a familiar sensation gripped me.

"What is it?" she asked.

I was frozen. She reached out to take the coin, but when her hand touched mine, she stopped.

"Something's happening, I can feel it! What is this? What's going on?"

"It's Conexus," I whispered. "I can sense the professor, somehow."

I'm certain that Olivia, in that moment, didn't entirely understand why this was shocking to me: Spindlebrock had informed us that the coin was made by Brevig, not himself! Why could I sense him? His statements and the reality of what I was feeling simply did not add up. Perhaps she may have connected those dots, but her mind was racing in another direction.

"Wait! I have an idea. Hold the token, like this—"

She rotated my wrist so that my hand was palm up.

"Open your hand, flat—like that. OK, now don't move."

Still holding my wrist, she began her incantation again. As she spoke, I focused on the professor; he was calm, but there was an anxiety in him—not the kind that is fearful, but the kind that is expectantly waiting to see how things will turn out.

Something started to happen, a vibration in my hand that felt like a warmth—at least, I thought it was in my hand at first, but the more I focused on it the more I understood that it was coming from Olivia's hand. My mouth gaped involuntarily as a copy of the token (I'm not sure how else to describe it) rose from the original. Olivia swayed as if moved on by some force—and in the middle of all this I saw what looked like a ghost passing right through the closed castle gate!

I gasped, and she opened her eyes; but I could see that her determination was still fixed. She too watched this apparition, as she finished the incantation. When it had passed all the way through the solid wood of the gate and into the bailey, she stopped, let go of my wrist, and grasped the ethereal coin that was floating in front of her. Then, she held it out to the ghost.

"Hello, professor. Here's the coin."

Chapter 17

Heta Padrobka

What strange languor or paralysis of the mind must have seized me, or perhaps it was in part due to the traditional Belarusian garb he wore—even so, how could I not recognize even for a moment, the professor who was to me the best friend in the world? As soon as Olivia spoke, the hypnosis was broken and I knew it was him, though I could scarcely believe his ghostlike appearance.

He reached out and took the coin from her hand, placing it in his pocket. He glanced at the coin in my hand. Knowing me as he does—apparently no matter what state he is in—Spindlebrock addressed me first.

"Thomas," he said, and his distant voice sent chills down my spine. "Time is short, I will explain all when this is over. Follow Olivia, and follow me. I will need you, just as much as I need her."

Then, turning to Olivia.

"I knew you could do it, and I thank you. You don't know what this means to me. Now go, and bid. Any amount, just keep bidding."

And with these words, he disappeared. I started to exhale a groan of panic and dread, but Olivia elbowed me in the stomach.

"Hand me that token, and keep your head on straight—they're up to thirty-four now, that means the scroll must be next!"

She was all but dragging me into the hall where the auction was taking place, and just in time. As we entered, Lot thirty-five was announced.

"Lot thirty-five. The fabled Kingmaker Scroll of Rognvald Eysteinsson. Created by said famous magician in Norway around the tenth century, this scroll has long been rumored to hold the secrets of eternal life."

I might have drawn undue attention to myself with the excessively audible gasp I let out, were it not for the fact that most of the audience responded in kind. The auctioneer commenced the bidding at an amount that sounded like more money than I could hope to earn in a dozen lifetimes. Countless hands went up, as did Olivia's, clutching Brevig's token.

Before long, the initial bid was doubled, and about half the original bidders were no longer raising their hands. Tripled, quadrupled, and more, and only a few hands were left. Obscene amounts of money were now being pledged, and before long, only three hands were still finding the courage to rise to what must represent the trading of their fortunes for the possibilities the scroll presumably held: Olivia, an unknown young woman in the front who also held up a Signum Dominii, and a man of middle-eastern descent nearer to us in the back.

The bidding continued, until the man in the back stood up, cursed all present, and left the building.

"We are down to two bidders," announced the auctioneer; and he seemed ready to proceed, when a voice, loud and distant, as if shouting from the top of one of the castle walls, broke in.

"Heta padrobka! Fake! Heta padrobka!"

And all of a sudden, Spindlebrock appeared, semi-transparent and scarcely connected to the balustrade on which he stood.

Utter astonishment froze the entire audience, but Glebovich didn't miss a beat. He rose and stormed right through Spindlebrock from behind, not seeing or recognizing his face.

"Please, be calm everyone. Please! This is nothing more than a harmless pryvid, an apparition of a person who lived long ago. They cannot see us, they cannot hear us, they cannot hurt us. The voice who claimed padrobka was most probably our noble friend who was just outbid. Come in here! Don't shout your accusations from outside, my friend!"

But the semi-disembodied voice, which the rapt audience could now place as actually coming from this apparition, repeated itself behind Glebovich.

"It is not him, but I, Professor C.C. Spindlebrock, who makes the accusation of padrobka. That scroll is a fake."

Glebovich's nostrils flared and his eyes widened as he recognized the voice. He spun around, and grabbed wildly at Spindlebrock, screaming profanities in his native tongue; but his arms passed through him. He motioned for his personal guards clad in red, who advanced to surround; but the professor was nothing they could capture. When the men gave up trying to take hold of him, he spoke again.

"To all present here, I now make an official claim that this scroll is not the famed Rognvald Scroll. I call on—"

But here, Glebovich cut him off with his booming voice.

"Stop at once! You have no place here—you are not here! You cannot make such a claim!"

Spindlebrock eyed him, apparently waiting to see if he would say more. The only sound in the room was a cough in the back, made by the man who had left but who had now returned to see what all the commotion was about.

"The House of Glebovich, unwilling to hear out a claim of heta padrobka, no matter who made it? In all the generations of your family, not once has any been afraid to hear the—"

"Enough!"

Glebovich's look was so furiously intense that I was surprised Spindlebrock—or whatever it was of him that we were seeing—didn't burst into flames. He spoke with a calm clarity that seemed intended to conceal his obvious rage.

"You shall not live, if alive you are, to insult my family's name even one more time. This I have already vowed, and this I shall ensure."

He dared Spindlebrock to speak, and finding no challenge, he motioned for his guards to sit while he turned and addressed the audience.

"Friends, a serious claim has been made. And though it was made not by one present, but by one who has illegally inserted himself in this place by some impossible means— yet we will honor it. Therefore, the House of Glebovich will give twenty four hours for proof to be provided showing that this item is not genuine, after which time—"

"I am prepared to prove my claim immediately," Spindlebrock broke in. "And in a way that even you cannot argue with. There are two gold bands, wrapped tightly around the base of each of your wands."

The face of the tyrannical host changed. Anger melted into anguish as he slowly turned toward Spindlebrock. The professor rushed to continue.

"I mean you no wrong today, Glebovich. I pour no salt in old wounds. We have been enemies, perhaps, but not everything has to end the way it starts. I'm entirely serious—in fact, I hope that after today, you will view me once again as a friend, if that is possible between us. Belarusian legend has long held that those bands, when worn by one who has the power that they focus, can uncover any forgery. They were made by your family, and worn by them for a time; they were what made this the most trusted auction house in the world.

"But the power to use them is not passed down from parent to child as was once supposed. You know this well, and now they are only a symbol. A symbol of your family's honor, magical ability, and duty—as you see it—to the people you serve. I am here to prove to you and the world, that the legends of your family and of your country are all true. Thomas Martin, come forward!"

I had not expected to hear my name, and for a brief moment I joined the crowd in looking around to see who he might be talking to. Realization broke on me, and before I knew what I was doing, I was awkwardly making my way to the balustrade. All eyes were of course fixed on me—even the still anguished eyes of that mountain of a man, Glebovich—but I had only one focus: Spindlebrock. What was he thinking? What was he doing? Why couldn't he have warned me, informed me, planned with me? My gaze was fixed on him as I marched down the center aisle and onto the balustrade.

"Some here may have heard of this man—my friend. His power and abilities are not a secret; he has proven himself to the commonality, even if not all choose to believe what they have heard. He has another gift, adjunct to the one for which he is known. Thomas, hold out your hands."

I was incredulous, and had no idea if he was serious or if he was bluffing, but I did as he commanded.

"Thank you—Glebovich, this can only proceed if you allow it; the gold bands from your wands, if you please."

He stared at us both until my arms began to tire. I wasn't sure how much longer I could hold them up, when all at once his resolve seemed to meld with the Professor's; he took out his wands, flipped the handles outward and held them in my direction.

"They are loose enough," was all he said.

"Take them, Thomas, and place one on each of your thumbs."

I obeyed. The gold rings were heavy, thick, and came off the ends of his wands with only a little effort.

"The spell please, Glebovich—you'll find that I am, in this state, powerless to affect anyone here physically or even with magic; just as you are powerless to affect me."

He flipped the wands once more, and placed the tip of each wand on a ring. With a simple spell, the rings tightened to a perfect fit.

"Steady, Thomas, there is no danger. Are they ready?"

Glebovich nodded. Then, in an effort that seemed to require all of his focus, he started on a lengthy incantation in a language that I could not place.

"It is finished, but this is not all that we will need. What of the dokaz? This was passed down to my brother, and I am afraid that it was lost to my family after that."

He looked genuinely ashamed at this admission. I imagined that he felt that this loss was, perhaps, the cause of his family's inability to perform whatever magic Spindlebrock thought I would be able to now manage.

"The dokaz is perhaps not what you think, Glebovich, or perhaps the mystery of it was never revealed to you. But in this thing I have seen and learned much. I always view legend as a way of preserving the truth, and the magical legends of Belarus gathered from sources far and wide, have sat upon the desk in my study for months at a time over the years. The dokaz is not lost; unlike the rings it is something that may be re-created over and over again, and it may be almost any object. One stipulation is this: the dokaz only works if it was created with very deliberate intent, and with emotion. The creator must have poured their heart and soul into it."

I was paying close attention to these proceedings in which I was playing, by Spindlebrock's design, such a pivotal part. When he said these words my mind snapped into focus; if we were dealing with objects made with this sort of intentionality, at least something related to Conexus seemed like a possibility.

"Your magical guard," Spindlebrock continued, motioning to the soldiers that still surrounded us, "are well known throughout the world. But even in their high ranks, there are levels. I believe that we will find our dokaz among them. Glebovich, will you instruct your guard to obey a few simple commands which I will give them? I ask that they will listen only to those commands that can cause no harm or danger to you, themselves, or your auction."

He motioned his consent toward one who appeared to be their captain; he in turn gave a few brief words of command in Belarusian to the others.

"As you know, many magicians buy their wands from master craftsmen—this is true all over the world, and is very much the expectation of most magicians. Yet some still make their own wands. Will those who crafted their own wands please step forward."

By quick count, about fifteen stepped forward.

"Those who responded, please come and make a line on the back of the balustrade. Very good. Those who harvested the wood with their own hands to make their wand—please remain on the stand. All others, please leave the stand and rejoin your fellows."

Roughly half vacated the balustrade.

"If the wand you now carry is the first wand you made in this way, using that wood which you harvested yourself, please also rejoin your fellows."

Four were left; the captain and the two that had been by his side all along (I'm not sure whether they stayed planted in defiance, or if they really did fit the criteria that Spindlebrock was laying out), and a much smaller and younger magician who looked as if he felt to be presuming wildly in his current position of attention.

Spindlebrock walked in front of the captain (Floated? Glided? It didn't seem entirely like walking) and addressed him directly.

"Describe very briefly how you made your wand."

He did so. It was a desiccated tale composed only of facts—where he went to get the wood, why the tree seemed most suitable, how he cut, stored, and dried it. He blandly described how he carved, and finished it to a plain, technical perfection.

Spindlebrock looked down, and said nothing. After a few moments of thought, he raised his head, and deliberately made his way past the other two guards and to the young man. He made the same request.

The young man was nervous, but he stood at attention, and shared his tale. His father was a wand maker by trade. They had gone together dozens of times to gather wood, and he had learned from him how to identify the best woods for different types of wands and different types of magicians. He had hand-carved or lathe-turned, and hand finished many wands under his father's instruction—but the wand he now carried, he had started working on the day of his father's death. On hearing the news of his passing, he had gone into the woods alone to seek solace; but the trees would not let him rest. He saw in every swaying monolith the image of his father, and the materials for making the best wands that man could want. The strain was too much, and he decided that he could not carry on his father's work; it was too painful. In tears, he gathered the wood for the last wand he would ever make, and the one that he now carried.

The young soldier paused, unable to continue. Spindlebrock attempted to truncate the tale for him.

"You finished it, trained with it, and took up work in the House of Glebovich, one of the oldest and most renowned magical establishments in the world. I have no doubt but that it is one of the most powerful wands a magician could hope to carry."

He nodded.

"What is your name?"

"Lukhym Navumcyk."

"Lukhym, will you allow us to use your wand for a few minutes? I promise it will be returned to you unharmed."

The young man, looking forward over the crowd and into space, produced the wand and presented it handle-first to Spindlebrock.

"I cannot take it; Thomas, please take the wand."

The young man step-rotated as I approached, and presented the wand to me. As I took it in my hands, I knew immediately that it was in fact an object crafted by the young man in front of me, and that it was made with more emotion than I had ever recognized in any object before or since. The sensation was so wildly intense, in fact, that I questioned what exactly was going on.

"Repeat these words, Thomas: 'This is the wand of Thalora Hex.'"

There was a single audible gasp in the audience, which drew the attention of everyone. I followed the eyes of those who had heard the sound more closely than I had—and saw them fixed on Evalyn, who was seated in the third row, dressed in traditional Belarusian garb. Her terrified eyes were fixed on me.

I was rattled, but Spindlebrock was unphased.

"It is the wrong name, and it doesn't matter at all. Just any old name. You see, dokaz means proof—proof that your ability is true. We take a known object, one that all present can trace to its owner, and you use it to demonstrate your power in the negative; you must first show the result of a false statement. Please repeat the words, 'This is the wand of Thalora Hex.'"

I repeated the words. The rings burned, and I felt a sinking feeling in my gut, as if the weight of some horrendous lie was gripping my soul.

"Don't let go! Hold the wand!"

I heeded Spindlebrock's commands, but the burning was increasing. I winced in pain, and was about to protest, when a visible light suddenly burst from the gold rings, illuminating the balustrade with a sickly red glow.

"Dokaz! It is proven! Just as the tales said!" Glebovich blurted out triumphantly.

The professor interrupted Glebovich's rejoicing with further instruction to me.

"It is but half proven! Thomas, say the words, 'This is the wand of Lukhym Navumcyk.'"

As quickly as I could, I belted out this new and true statement. The pain stopped, the burning was instantly cooled, and the red light transformed into a luster and sheen that wasn't really a rainbow, but which seemed to be every color individually yet all at once. The entire hall glowed with this powerful light.

"There," said Spindlebrock after a moment. "Now it is proven. The rings, the charm, the dokaz, and the magician are all in place. We can now prove any challenge of heta padrobka, in the old Belarusian way—in the Glebovich way."

Chapter 18

The Truth About the Scroll

For me these proceedings were fantastic. Throughout all this—apart from the exclamation that revealed the presence of Evalyn—the audience was almost entirely silent. The events were, it seemed, abnormal enough to keep the attention of all present.

After the dokaz exercise was complete, a palpable wave of relief swept over the crowd, who became suddenly chatty. Babble, whisper, and gossip were exchanged freely; though I later learned that this sort of behavior would not normally have been tolerated in the least. Glebovich himself was beaming, almost beside himself with pride and wonder at this validation of his family's stories, honor, and renown. Evalyn alone remained stony-faced, her gaze ever fixed on me.

It wasn't long before the intangible manifestation of Spindlebrock got Glebovich's attention, whispering to him at length. After this exchange, the latter regained control of his environment.

"Friends and guests!" his voice boomed over the clatter. "Please remember the import and weight of the event you have been invited to attend!"

Silence and decorum returned.

"I have been reminded by the professor that we have not yet addressed the claim of heta padrobka which he has raised. The auction cannot go forward if the item can be proven a fake.

"Also," he continued, "though some believe that the House of Glebovich knowingly allows stolen items to come to this block—"

He paused and cast a glance of defiance at Spindlebrock.

"—I will remind you that in the ancient rules which govern this auction, which are in the book you all signed, it is stated that if the rings can demonstrate true ownership— which is just one aspect of their legendary powers—then the House of Glebovich will return that item to its rightful owner."

The whispers started again, but stopped almost as quickly with one glance from the commanding master of ceremonies. Seeing that all was understood, he motioned for the professor to speak.

"Thomas, please take the scroll from the auctioneer."

The wide-eyed auctioneer, after glancing at Glebovich for permission, took the scroll carefully off the block and placed it gently in my open hands. It was lighter than I thought it would be, and looked to be made from a sort of thin parchment. It was tied with two leather straps, which were held in place by two cut gemstone-like beads. But there was something else about it that troubled me exceedingly.

"Thomas, repeat after me: 'This is a simple scroll of enchantment, for cleaning a bathroom.'"

There was a short burst laughter from the audience, forcefully abbreviated by the searching eye of Glebovich, who did not find the solemn occasion of restoring his family honor amusing.

I repeated the words; the pain, the red glow—this assertion about the scroll was a lie. I knew it, everyone knew it.

"Again, repeat after me: 'This is an authentic, original, complex scroll filled with powerful runes and deep magic.'"

I repeated. The red grew deeper and brighter, and the pain more intense, and the lie was proven. The professor hastened to continue.

"Once again! Repeat: 'This is truly the fabled Kingmaker Scroll of Rognvald Eysteinsson.'"

Total silence fell; even breathing seemed to cease. As I repeated these words it is almost impossible to describe the blood-like quality of the red light that now emanated from the gold rings. Nor can I describe the hateful burning that seared my skin at their touch. I might have screamed, if my heart and mind and thoughts weren't entirely taken in by the events now unfolding.

"It is enough," the professor began quietly, "but it is not all that we can show here. Thomas, repeat these words now! 'This scroll is a cunning decoy, created and owned by Lucas Brevig. It was placed at the Cascabela by Professor C.C. Spindlebrock as a trap, to lure those who would dare challenge the real scroll's rightful owner."

Before I tell you what came next, I must clarify what it was about the scroll that troubled me so much as it was placed in my hands. Conexus, in this context, was being used to identify ownership and authenticity of an object, by detecting lies or truths about the object. Having been called upon several times by Glebovich, over the years that followed these events, I know that the rings allow me to use my gift on objects created both by those living, and by those who have passed on—something that I can't do without the rings. But the effects and experience are different. You'll recall that as I took Lukhym's wand, the more readily understood experience (for me at least) of connecting with the object's living owner, occurred instantly; I knew the wand was his. When I took this apparently fake scroll, I did not detect some connection to the largely mysterious Lucas Brevig, or to someone no longer living—I knew at once that this scroll had been created by the professor himself.

And so, when the professor asked me to say, "This scroll is a cunning decoy, created and owned by Lucas Brevig," I was confused. I knew it was not true. At first, I thought it was another lie that the rings would prove—but why fabricate a lie so close to the truth, and to prove what? What else needed to be shown and how was this to show it? I was so confused, I asked him to give me the words one more time. He did, and as I repeated them, I expected the red glow to become even more dire, and for the rings to draw actual blood from my hands—but the opposite effect, the one from before, replaced all the pain and darkness with a beautiful peace and luminous light.

My eyes met his, but that familiar and somewhat smug facial expression that meant, "trust me, and all your questions will be answered in time" was all I found.

At the visible change of the light, and the accompanying revelation of the truth, the crowd lost all control. People were standing up and shouting, arguing, frustrated and angry. Many of them, I supposed, had made the trip to the auction just to catch a glimpse of the famous scroll. And now, they realized that they had all been deceived.

At first, Glebovich was just as angry and dumbfounded as the rest. He made no effort to quell the commotion; he just stood there glued to the spot, dumb, his head shaking endlessly. Being near him, I could hear him muttering to himself.

"It's not possible. She assured me that this scroll was authentic—and she is no magician to be trifled with! This is not possible—she assured me."

Over the tumult, I also heard Spindlebrock address the great man.

"Glebovich, by the rules of your house, you must return the scroll to its rightful owner—which is me. Please allow Thomas to retain it in my place, as I am currently unable."

The dazed man only nodded. Spindlebrock motioned for me to place the scroll in a loose pocket at the front of my linen shirt, which I did. Commotion was transforming into pandemonium, and the captain of the guard finally spoke up, snapping Glebovich out of his reverie. He roared out a command, and silence followed. Slowly, he announced the end of the auction. He was about the perform the charm that would end this enchantment that we were collectively a part of, when the professor broke out:

"Stop her! She is implicated in the padrobka!"

He pointed to Evalyn, who was now stealthily making her way toward the back of the crowd. A man near her reached out, but she evaded his grasp. Magician after magician literally jumped at the chance of being able to capture one responsible for so great a fiasco; yet she dodged them all, dipping and diving and jumping like an acrobat.

"Enough!"

I had heard Spindlebrock use that word in exactly that tone once before. For a brief moment the memory of Talbot, the day we found him, came back to me—but here and now, I knew the professor couldn't do a thing. He had already admitted as much to Glebovich; he could not affect anyone present by means magical or physical.

And yet, he broke into a complex spell. It was, I thought, not unlike the one that Glebovich had used to open the auction.

Reality changed around us. Those who were still seated in chairs tumbled to the ground as the chairs disappeared. The building we were in seemed to flicker and fade in sections; chunks of the roof were gone, windows that were whole were now shattered or missing, pieces of the walls were gaping open to the bailey outside. Through one of these holes, I saw that the walls were now in a state of ruin— not total ruin and partial repair as they were when we had arrived, but not whole again as we had seem them with Glebovich's transformation.

"No! How can this—Stop! Not now, not this—you are a madman!"

It was Glebovich addressing Spindlebrock. But the professor continued, and the charm was completed. Its impacts had even stopped Evalyn in her tracks. With Glebovich's initial spell, the castle had been restored to some former glory, a time of wholeness. Now, it looked as if it were in the middle of a war zone. I barely had time to take it in, when I learned that my initial impression was perhaps not wrong.

A high-pitched whine that got closer. An impact; an explosion. It hit on the outside of the castle wall with a deafening burst, and before anyone really understood what was going on, stones and bricks were raining down on us.

"Quickly Thomas, to Evalyn!"

And with this, he suddenly disappeared. Without thought, I darted forward and jumped from the balustrade. I heard a guard cry out for me to stop, but as I turned I witnessed a piece of rubble hitting Glebovich in the head—and I shutter to describe it, but it appeared that the rubble actually passed through his head somehow, similar to how Spindlebrock passed through the gate. The focus of his guards was now absorbed in rescuing their leader, and I fled unchallenged. I could not see Evalyn through the chaos, but I made my way toward the back where I had last seen her. Finally, I caught a glimpse of her, crumpled on the ground with the professor and Olivia hunched over her. Olivia seemed, I thought, to be taking her pulse.

"Come quick! Take Olivia's other hand!" was the professor's next instruction.

I did so, and instantly experienced a sensation of vibration throughout my entire body. And then, we began to sink.

"Don't let go! Do not let go! I'll meet you there."

We were sinking, and I did not let go. My legs were in the ground—literally in the ground—and I could not move them. Now my waist, and next my chest. I held my breath instinctively, as my head passed under the earth, but I could not close my eyes.

Perhaps it sounds ridiculous—even more unbelievable than what I've already shared—but in this state Evalyn, Olivia, and I all passed through the dirt and rock of the bailey, and into a long cave passage below.

"There," Olivia said. "It's done—you can let go now Thomas."

It was dimly lit, but enough for me to see that we were not alone. There were others here—people, yet not quite. They were like the professor, ghost-like and transparent. And even more strange to my eyes, they seemed to be dressed in more modern clothing—military clothing! Were these soldiers? Of what war, what time?

"They can't see us," were the words of Professor Spindlebrock, "and we don't have much time. Glebovich will awaken, and he will end this journey—this will hurt, Thomas, but the rings will help you focus I think. I don't think you'll pass out like last time, especially since she is not conscious."

He motioned, and I understood; he wanted me to take hold of Evalyn's hand, as I had in Bardo's restaurant. I drew a deep breath, and took her hand in mine.

Chapter 19

The Truth About Evalyn

I did not black out, but the pain forced my eyes closed as I winced; and when they shut, I found myself elsewhere, and nowhere. What I experienced defies actual description to a degree, as it did not feel quite conscious, waking, and real. The best I can do with words is to say that I found myself in an entirely black room—but the blackness was not in color, it was more of an emptiness or void. There were no walls, ceiling, or floor. Nothing to stand on, nothing to see around me—I was simply there. And I was not alone.

Nearby, I found Evalyn. She appeared to be lying down (though on what, or where, I could not say), sleeping peacefully.

"She is unconscious."

It was a woman's voice. I looked around, and saw her walking toward me—from her build and her gait, I knew immediately that she was the person from the surveillance videos I had watched so many times, the burglar who stole into the Cascabela that night, along the top of the outer wall.

"What is this?"

I could have started with a thousand different questions, I suppose, but this is what came out of my mouth—or my mind; I'm not sure if I even spoke the words.

"This is the soul of Evalyn Reyes."

"The soul?"

"Yes, or the mind, heart, spirit, consciousness, subconscious, essence—take your pick. I call it her soul. This is the state where thought becomes action, the animation of the physical body."

"How are we here?"

"Well, I know how I am here. What I don't know is how you are here. I knew something was wrong, that day you took hold of her hand in that hotel. You see, I felt you here, in her soul."

"So how are you here, then?"

As I came to grips with the complex realities that were being opened, part of me struggled to keep a grip on the actualities of my situation—somewhere, I was with Olivia, Evalyn, and the professor, and they were waiting for me. To do what? I grappled with the question of what I was supposed to accomplish.

"That's a trade secret, darling. Perhaps you already know? Your professor probably has an idea, as he usually does. At first, I thought that after Adana, you both knew about this—arrangement. I thought you had found me out. But time went by and nothing happened."

"How could it?" I ventured.

Here she looked at me searchingly, her eyes narrowed. I looked back, attempting with all my might to project a confidence that I did not possess.

"Perhaps he could do nothing, or would do nothing. Perhaps he doesn't care—but I know him well enough. He's like you, though he doesn't show it."

As she spoke, she circled me like I was prey. Her movements were graceful, even cat-like.

"Then an opportunity came along; and I never miss an opportunity."

"The scroll," I guessed, suppressing any emotion in my voice.

"Yes, the scroll. Lowen was always so reckless. I remember when I was like him, you know. He wanted everything, and he thought he knew how to get it. It was so delightful for me, to string him along. I actually laughed when he asked."

I was taken aback by the mention of Lowen, having expected another name. But I kept my composure—if only Spindlebrock could be around when I was able to keep it together, then he could perhaps learn to trust my so-called acting skills! I kept my silence, and waited for her to reveal more.

"You see, so little pleases me at this point—ask the professor about that sometime. We all have our amusements. I took the job, just for the thrill of it. And with Evalyn on the inside—"

Here she laughed.

"It was twice as fun. No one ever questions my methods, so I was left to do as I pleased. And what I wanted was all of this; the chaos, the suspense, the intrigue, the attention—well, most of it."

She stopped, and looked at the sleeping Evalyn.

"You can see, I hadn't quite planned on certain things. C.C. is like that, you know, he tends to get in the way. But it doesn't matter. If it comes to it—but there's no need, he would never—ah, look!"

Evalyn was beginning to stir.

"Well, I suppose that is that and we'll see what comes next. For now, I believe we are done."

She folded her arms and looked at me intently. I was searching for something more to say when a sudden searing pain pierced my mind. I didn't really feel it in my body (I don't think I felt anything in my body in that state), but it caused such excruciating pain that I ceased to perceive.

Chapter 20

More Than They Realize

I awoke in the dingy inn where we had slept earlier that day. Someone had changed me back into my own clothes, and laid me out on a couch in the sitting room. The tabby cat named Penny was curled up and purring contentedly on my chest.

Olivia and Spindlebrock were standing nearby, speaking with Glebovich and two of his guards. Lukhym stood in a corner, looking uncomfortable and out of place. I saw the professor set the two gold rings in Glebovich's hands. The two embraced.

"Where's Evalyn?" I asked.

"Ah, Thomas, you're awake! She escaped, I'm afraid. I'll tell you all about it."

The professor was back to his usual, tangible self.

"Thomas Martin," interrupted Glebovich. "I had no idea that one day I would meet such a magician as you! I've promoted Lukhym to carry the dokaz, as my brother once did. It is my sincere hope that you will return again sometimes to Kreva, that I may call upon you both in such rare cases as may come to present themselves in the future."

He looked around the room.

"But next time, you will stay with me in my home."

I consented, assuring him that I would be ready to help him any time I could. After all, it was in the interest of the truth; and the experience, though taxing, was of such a rare nature that I couldn't say no to the thought of being a part of it again.

After he and his men departed, I implored the professor and Olivia to fill me in on what had occurred between the time I took Evalyn's hand, and the time I woke up in the inn.

"When you touched her, you passed out," Olivia began. "Evalyn woke up immediately after that—and she didn't waste any time. She really must be a telekinetic, because she lifted me in the air without a thought, and threw me into the darkness."

"I could do nothing, Thomas," added Spindlebrock. "Evalyn fled as swiftly, quietly, and nimbly as a cat; so I followed Olivia to see that she was not hurt."

"We had to get out of there," she continued. "The professor had shifted Glebovich's spell—well, maybe you had better explain it professor, I'm not sure I understand everything."

"Very well. The house is secure, and we are the only ones here at present—apart from the cat—so we can speak freely. Like I mentioned earlier, I was not allowed in at the auction;

Glebovich and I were not on good terms. What you just witnessed, before he parted, was the resolution of hard feelings that have existed between us for a long, long time.

"Glebovich's auction takes place—as you surely already guessed—in a confluence. That hotel in Turkey was also in a similar, specific portion of a confluence. The spell that I command in that place is capable of transporting anyone at that table into the past, to a time when that hotel was bustling with magicians.

"But don't misunderstand—you cannot travel to the past, not in the sense that you might think. You can go there, and observe, and be acted upon by the past to a degree, but you cannot go to the past and act, or influence anything or anyone. What is done, is done, and cannot be changed. But it can be observed. Had you risen from the table in that place, in that state—you would have been trapped, and unable to act fully and freely in any time or place."

He sighed.

"I digress; the Kreva castle is in a similar portion of a more powerful confluence. Glebovich commands a spell that only his family knows, which can shift the entire castle back through time. In this way, he is able to give his auction-goers the experience that you had, of witnessing the castle in its full glory. It is both impressive, and secure, as it is supposed to prevent anyone from entering the auction after it starts—they not being a part of the spell.

"Which is where Olivia came in. With her gift, I believed that she would be able to bring me into the castle. She has been rapidly developing skills in elemental magic that many can't fathom at all, and that very few will ever witness. I still believe that given enough time and the right circumstances, she could have done it on her own—but perhaps I was mistaken. She informed me that you two worked together, in a way that is entirely outside the realms of my personal research and understanding."

I only nodded. The fact was, it was beyond my understanding as well.

"Therefore, using what Sanjay has taught her so far, coupled with some kind of interaction of your gifts, she brought me in; but though she could shift my phase enough to be present, she could not match me entirely to the surroundings. This I expected and planned on, actually, and I believe it rather helped than hurt matters. In the state you saw me—like a ghost, you might say—I was unable to act or be acted upon by anyone or anything physically present. Glebovich couldn't touch me, or cast a spell on me, for example. Quite important, considering our past.

"This explains the state of things up to a point, I hope. When Evalyn was attempting to escape, I knew that there was little chance of stopping her without some decisive action. I could take no physical action, so what was left? While I do not know how to perform the exact spell that can move the castle through time—I hope you understand just how impressive that spell is, Thomas, it's not something that you just pick up—I do know enough about the theories of the magic involved to cast a spell to alter it; and I was willing to try. I was planning on being ready for such an eventuality, in point of fact, and had studied out the fine details of my methods very carefully. You were not in clumsy hands.

"My spell bumped the castle forward through time only slightly. If you know the history of that castle, you know that it was on the front lines in the First World War. A time of chaos and bombardment, as you witnessed. If I could not stop her, then perhaps the chaos could—I will explain.

"As the guests entered the castle grounds, they arranged themselves quite on purpose, as you saw. Their arrangement was incredibly specific; there were markers on the ground. As Glebovich cast the spell, they all sat down— there were no chairs before the spell, those were part of the past, you see?"

I did not see, and he knew it.

"The physical surroundings of the past, in that place, were like the confluence table in a certain sense. There is a spell on the Kreva castle like there is a spell on the tables in the Mazi. It is a connection that draws objects through time and space. I have absolutely no idea how an entire castle was enchanted that way, or why, but I know it is thus.

"And, just as you could sit at that table in the ruined hotel, and travel back to a different time still interacting with that table, you could interact with the physical materials from the past in the castle—rather, they could interact with you, I should say. I mean, by that, that though you could perhaps sit on a chair, or be hit by a rock or brick from the castle wall—you could not hope to act on those objects. You could not move a chair, or deflect a rock or brick. You simply cannot alter the past."

"But—then a rock might fly right through you!"

I couldn't help blurting out the thought. I recalled what I had seen, but not understood, when it happened to Glebovich.

"No, not exactly. The amount of force, the extent of the interaction, is limited. Enough to sit on a chair and be upheld, enough to be hurt by a rock—but the elements are not bound enough for a rock to go through a person, not in the destructive physical sense. The phase-connection breaks, the rock passes through on its unaltered and historically-deterministic course, and only acts on you to a degree. It hurts, but cannot kill. A bullet or a bomb would be the same, actually. Sort of like when Glebovich tried to grab me—he passed through. We were disconnected, out of phase enough so that grabbing me was not possible."

My head was starting to ache, but by accepting without really understanding, I comprehended what he meant at least in part.

"And so, to answer your original question of what happened after you passed out: Evalyn awoke and escaped, and Olivia and I were left to manage things, you being unconscious. Glebovich was about to awaken from the bump he received, cast the spell to end the phase shift on the castle, and bring everyone back to that thing we call the present. Olivia brought us back to the surface—I neglected to tell you, her phase shifting was what let us pass through solid ground, to the tunnels they used during the war—and then she had to force me back to my normal phase. This is difficult with humans, as I think I've made clear—you have to have a strong connection to them, which is difficult if they are not with you, or in phase. With the new copy of the Signum Dominii, which was in phase, she was able to do this."

I thought about the token and the scroll and Brevig, and was going to interrupt, but he hastened to continue.

"With that token we had a connection; She moved me out of that state before Glebovich completed his spell."

"It was a stupid risk," Olivia broke in. "Sanjay warned me about the kinds of things that can happen if this stuff goes wrong. You could have been trapped forever!"

"Yes, but I assumed that risk, and I was willing—"

"It was my risk too! You think I want to be responsible for trapping you in some phase of time, ruining your life?"

Spindlebrock hung his head.

"I'm sorry; I really wouldn't wish that on anyone. But thank you for doing what you did—I believed that you could. And I honestly was willing to take the risk. It was critically important to me, now that you've started down this path, to see what you might be capable of—please, I know it sounds selfish, but I have my reasons, Olivia, just as you do."

Neither continued, so after a long silence, I spoke up.

"And so, that explains a lot about what happened, and how it happened. But what was the purpose? Why chase a fake scroll, and risk so much? What did we gain out of all this?"

Spindlebrock perked up, a fresh optimism in his face.

"So much more than you could possibly realize! And with you two working together, what else could be possible? It's staggering to think of. And what we gained might be even more than what I'm thinking of, if you saw anything at all when you touched Evalyn's hand—did you?"

I related all I had seen and experienced, in what was apparently only a moment of time for them both. The professor looked grave, but not surprised.

"Absolutely fascinating."

"Do you have any idea what was going on? She seemed to think you might."

"I believe I do, but it would be quite difficult to explain right now. She implicated Lowen, you say?"

"Well, she mentioned Lowen being reckless, then said she 'took the job', which in my mind meant she took it from him."

"Which means we need to get back to India to determine if there is any truth in that."

"But professor, who in the world was this woman? She claimed that we were in the 'soul' of Evalyn, and that she had recognized me there at Bardo's—she knew about that on her own, I didn't mention it—how could she be there? How could I be there? What was she doing to her?"

"I don't know for certain, but I am beginning to get a firmer grip on the threads of it. Could you identify this woman, if you ever saw her again?"

"I will never forget her. But, was she real?"

"I'll see what I can do about giving you the chance to find out for yourself. For the moment, we need to get back to the Black Cascabela. Based on what you've revealed, I think that Lowen will probably be waiting for us; I hope he has a better explanation than the one I've arrived at on my own."

Chapter 21

The Capture

We did not return to India via the same route that we used to leave it; the professor opted for a much slower method—flight—which he said would "help us clear our heads". He explained that he had already dispatched help to the Cascabela, to make sure things didn't go wrong there, and that he had requested the Preeminent Council's intervention, to help question Lowen and determine responsibility in the case of the burglary, with potential remediation if necessary.

For non-magician readers who may not be aware, I note here that the Preeminent Council is a profoundly private and secretive group. They employ an organization of magicians which they simply call "secretaries", located around the globe, to help them sort out which magical cases might truly need their attention. Those who wish to have the Council preside in a tribunal must appeal to the secretaries. The professor had done this over the phone in Kreva, and the request had been instantly granted. I assumed that Spindlebrock had encountered this council previously, but for Olivia and me this was to be the first time.

When we finally landed in Salem, India, there were two magicians waiting for us at the airport, to drive us to the casino. Spindlebrock seemed to know them, but introduced them only briefly as Tahlia and Leonardo. He used our drive to explain to them every detail he could fit into that short ride, concerning the scroll investigation and the auction. He was thorough and open, and I determined that he must have trusted those two wizards completely.

As we approached the casino, he outlined his plans for Lowen.

"Ultimately the Council will need to interrogate him. But I would like to have the opportunity to ask him a few questions before he is taken into custody—I'll go in with Thomas and Olivia, and explain things to him."

Tahlia and Leonardo seemed surprised by this arrangement, but did not offer any objection beyond their doubtful expressions.

"After we speak with him, I believe he'll deliver himself to the Council willingly. If he's not inclined, I'll make sure he is persuaded. We are here, let's go."

Taking his leave of Tahlia and Leonardo, Spindlebrock led the way, and we followed. We passed the front desk and entered the lobby, which was abandoned—or so we thought. As we began to pass through it, a voice came from a corner table.

"For some reason I thought you would come alone."

It was Lowen.

"I used to do almost everything alone. But I'm past that now," was the professor's reply.

"Please, come and sit. I had the lobby cleared out for our use when I learned that you were arriving. We won't be bothered here."

"They told you I was coming?"

"Not exactly, but I figured you would. They only told me that I was requested to remain on the premises for questioning related to the scroll. I learned of your flight on my own."

We seated ourselves at his table. His gaze followed only the professor.

"Remain on the premises means, 'Better not try to leave!' I think. I wasn't told who it was that wanted to question me, but I can guess."

"I requested the Preeminent Council, and they accepted. I'm to escort you to them."

"That sounds ominous. Aren't two council members required to come and fetch me? Isn't that the rule?"

"Maybe not a rule, but a custom. I told them that I wanted to ask you a few questions first."

I gathered by now, and I'm sure Olivia did as well, that the two wizards we had traveled with were members of the Preeminent Council, a pair of the most powerful magicians in the world.

"And why should I answer your questions? I suppose I could simply keep my mouth shut."

"There was enough evidence to convince the secretaries and activate the Council. They'll have their answers, Lowen. One way or another the truth will come out. I just thought you'd like to talk about it first—with us."

Lowen looked at him long and hard, then at me.

"It's tempting, it really is. I could simply disappear, though."

"No one can simply disappear, and if you had wanted to try you would have done that when we left the casino. At this point, it would be almost impossible. Even if you could get away from us and those waiting for you outside, where would you go? You'd have to start an entirely new life, which is no simple task."

"Simpler for some than for others, I think. Well, you are right about one thing—I would like to talk to you. Oh, I have plenty to say to you! The problem is, I suspect that you already know a great deal of what I'm going to say. I'm a bit disappointed in the way things turned out."

"You're talking about Evalyn."

"I am. I heard from two of my sources at the auction that you took her, after some rather impressive magical performances. You have, I presume, interrogated her."

"We have," he lied.

"I'm surprised you caught her, she was very adept—wait, I guess I did hear that she was unconscious when you took her, so I suppose that explains it. Was obtaining a confession difficult?"

"For any other magician it might have been, but for me it was quite manageable."

"Well, no one is perfect. She is a very talented magician —confusingly so, especially in her ability to withstand potions—but who can resist Professor Spindlebrock? Do you mind telling me, is she safe and secure now? I just want to know that she's alright. We worked together for a long time."

"Yes, she is."

"That's good. You know, she told me that the mundus potion she took in Adana was just water? But I don't actually believe her. I have no idea how she escaped from that situation. Did you know, I could never seem to clear her memory, or hide from her? It was a mystery to me. Never quite felt like I had a hold on that one."

Could it be? Lowen was now referencing events in Turkey—events connected to—could it be?

"Maybe you never did have a hold on her."

"Perhaps, but my potions are—effective."

"Effective is not the same as comprehensive. There are things about Evalyn that you may not have understood."

"There was a lot about Evalyn that I didn't understand. But that is all in the past now, and it's not likely that I ever will understand, given that you have her, and she has now revealed all."

"No, not all. She couldn't tell us why you chose the name. What does it mean?"

"Crane?"

Lowen had spoken the word. Spindlebrock had carefully drawn it out of him, proving by him saying it first that this conversation was really what it sounded like. Somehow, this man before us was also—

"William Cartwright Crane," Lowen said thoughtfully.

All was confusion for me, but I sat as still as stone. Olivia was equally petrified.

"He was an ancestor of mine, and early magician who lived just after the Revolutionary War. He led a faction of magicians that were tired of the rest of humanity having a say in government, while we were forced to sit idly by. I thought it might be ironic, I suppose. Or poetic. Now you tell me: Why Spindlebrock?"

The professor looked confused at the question—and somewhere beneath the surface, angry.

"It's the name my mother gave me."

"Yes, I know—once upon a time. Well, then, why Brevig? Or Morgan, or Andrews, or Robles? Why not just Spindlebrock, Spindlebrock, Spindlebrock all the time?"

He was on the edge of his seat, agitated, his voice rising.

"Thomas Martin," he said suddenly, turning to me. "I suppose that is your real name?"

"Y-Yes."

"You know, I had so many ideas of how you could be useful to me! I guess the professor beat me to it—boy did you beat me to it Spindlebrock! I heard that in Kreva, you identified the scroll as a fraud, a fake. The whole audience could see your power on display, legendary power not seen for who knows how long. But what did you feel, when you held that scroll?"

"That's enough, Lowen," interrupted the professor.

"Why? You know, I'm going to pay for what I've done—yes, what I've done. I don't blame you, no matter what I wrote."

He faltered as he referenced the letter he wrote to Spindlebrock and me after the death of Talbot.

"No, I don't blame you here at the end, when nothing can stop it. I'm no spineless, sentimental fool. I was afraid when he died... afraid that I was to blame. I will pay, I know I will. But you're the one who wanted to talk—no, you wanted answers!"

He slammed his fist on the table.

"Well, I want them too! Why not let a man meet his doom with his curiosity satiated, his itches scratched?"

Spindlebrock looked at him, and I thought I saw real pity in his eyes.

"Answer him, Thomas."

I told him that when I held the scroll, I felt that it had been created by Spindlebrock.

"That's what I thought. But didn't you speak the words, 'This scroll was created by Lucas Brevig'? That's what I was told by the two magicians I sent to keep an eye on Evalyn."

I nodded.

"And you thought, in that moment, 'If this is Spindlebrock's scroll, then why is it also Brevig's scroll?' right? Tell me that's not what you thought."

I confirmed that the thought had crossed my mind.

"And the professor, he owned right up and told you, didn't he?"

"We haven't had time—" I started.

"Haven't had time? No time? Was the auction five minutes ago? No time for a little chat, a little truth, eh Spindlebrock?"

The men eyed one another. Spindlebrock eventually spoke.

"What do you want, Lowen?"

"I want to reveal what you refuse to reveal to anyone! You won't tell these two—his closest friends I suppose he made you believe—and besides, I've got nothing to lose. Let's see if you'll let me tell them. Let's see if the words will drop from my lips before you take out your wand and silence me for good!"

He waited for a response, but none came. The professor looked calm, almost serene.

"This man, your Professor Spindlebrock, is a Sempiternus—he holds the secrets of eternal life, in that scroll, and he shares them with no one."

He looked at us all, in turn. I didn't know what to think, and Olivia didn't seem to either. Spindlebrock still looked peaceful.

"Spindlebrock! He was born Cyrus Cardamom Spindlebrock, around the year eighteen twenty. For fifty years he went by this name—oh yes, I've searched out your history and studied you for my entire adult life; I know your secrets. I'm not sure how or when, but at some point he obtained the scroll. He took on a supposed apprentice, by the name of Charles Morgan—just a pseudonym, he was in fact his own apprentice, in disguise! 'Spindlebrock' died a decade or two later. This Morgan eventually took on an apprentice by the name of Tobias Andrews, and his apprentice was Marius Robles—who was the magician that trained Lucas Brevig. All of these were really just one person, moving through the generations under different names."

He paused, daring any of us to interrupt.

"And then something happened. Lucas Brevig took on an apprentice, a Cyrus Cardamom Spindlebrock. Born again—except, he really never died. That fake scroll, the one supposedly made by Brevig; and the token that Olivia was waving around stupidly as I'm told, the one that represented Brevig and could only function as a Signum Dominii if Brevig himself had placed it into her hands! He didn't tell you both that? A Signum Dominii isn't something you can pass from person to person, it can only be given directly from the creator to the representative; one transfer, that is all it will withstand. I guess he made you think he was transferring it from Brevig to you! If you could find relics made by Morgan or Andrews or Robles, Thomas, they would tell you the same thing that scroll or that coin could: This man in front of you has never ceased being, for over two hundred years!"

Flustered and breathing rapidly, Lowen still held our total attention.

"Do you deny it?" he demanded.

"I'm impressed with even these sparse observations, Lowen, they must have been incredibly difficult to come by; I've been extremely discreet over the years. I never took you for a magician of substance, or a person who could pursue this kind of deep research with seriousness."

Lowen guffawed sardonically.

"You mock me, even as I reveal your most closely held secret! Now your secret will not die with me—and unless you plan on killing your friends, it will no longer be a secret."

"It is a relief to you and me both."

This was clearly not the response Lowen had been anticipating or desiring. He pushed his seat to the floor as he rose violently.

"I never was a magician of substance, as you put it! Money runs deep in my family, not magic. When I started I could barely flip a page in a book using a wand—surely you remember that. In fact, I was so bad off, my father hired a personal tutor, the most renowned magician in the world, he said. You showed up looking much the same age you look now, actually. You worked tirelessly on me, but eventually told my father that I should go into the family business instead of pursuing magic, so I could do something useful. You crushed his opinion of me, and relegated me to a lifetime of puerile grubbing after money.

"But even if talent was lacking, determination was never in short supply. I mastered enough of magic to get by. After you gave up on me, I learned everything there is to learn about potions. Where magical prowess and natural talent were lacking, I supplied the deficiency with effort piled upon effort, endlessly. Eventually, I learned that the kinds of potions I was capable of creating were worth more than any spell I might conjure up—more than just money and the petty swindles of a two-bit casino and resort world. As my skill grew, demand for my potions grew, and I knew what my first calling was in life. I moved through every circle of magicians—every circle!—and learned that there was a world, a whole world of magic that your precious universities don't even scratch the surface of.

"My second calling dawned on me gradually—I wanted to learn what made you, Professor C.C. Spindlebrock, the best magician in the world. What made magicians start and look over their shoulder at your name? I delved into science, and pursued the company of what one with an open mind might call more enlightened magicians. For a while I even considered myself your equal, and longed for you to share that opinion; I thought I could convince you. I eventually discovered information about the confluences, which you have studied extensively. Available knowledge was severely limited, but I exploited every source, and followed your trail of study to every end. In the process, I learned of the lineage of your master-apprentice relationships. You thought you had buried that trail, didn't you? I, a magician without substance, found it.

"I guessed you were a Sempiternus, but didn't know how you did it. For years I postulated that you were using the confluences to travel in time, or rather to slow time to somehow prolong your life. Yes, I even found the two distinct forms of the confluence, though I bet you thought that secret was yours alone. And, I could use some of the tables by that point, at least the ones that could be bought; but I knew that you were doing something else, something more. I'm sure you can appreciate the effort I made to follow your trail to Tribune.

"Ah, Tribune, Kansas! That place where you did so much of your research—oh yes, I learned all about your profound confluence studies, professor—which is why I put so much effort into finding the exact location where you carried them out. I tracked your confluence travels for years, through a network of spies, and learned that it was that one table that held the key. No one knew where it went, only that you used it regularly; but I followed you there to Tribune, through all that unfortunate nonsense and all those abductions.

"I brought the best magicians—well, the best corruptible ones—with me there once I knew were it was, and no magic was too dark in our pursuit of the secrets and memories that are imbued in the very walls and stones of that ancient dwelling place. You tried to conceal it with that old farm, but I was not fooled. We found the entrance, and together we broke the protective stones you placed there. And in the very essence of that place, to my great disappointment, I discovered what was for me a dead end. It was only raw science, the bare functionality of the confluences, that you pursued. Valuable, powerful, mystical, alluring—all of this and more—and yet nothing about the essence of life. It was Sempiternus that I was after—eternal life, the one thing we all want. The one thing I thought that if I somehow discovered on my own, would prove to you that I was worthy of being called your equal."

He paused, and the professor interjected.

"I'm dismayed that I caused you so much pain, Lowen. I probably cause many people a great deal of pain just by my nature, and you were young—but I can't answer for what you've done with your pain. You made others pay the price of your pursuits."

Lowen laughed.

"I'm sure that in your long life, you've learned all about that."

"I have, and I'll be accountable for my own choices. I have another curiosity, since you mentioned the abductions:

There was a cloak that you wore, when you abducted these young people—"

Lowen's eyes narrowed.

"Impossible. It's impossible that you could know about that."

"Perhaps—but that cloak, since we're scratching itches, was it the famed cloak of Saint Francis of Assisi?"

Lowen smiled dimly.

"It was. I'm impressed. And I promised myself that nothing you could do would ever impress me again. I should not have promised myself anything in relation to you."

"Well, I have to give credit to Olivia for that one. But tell me, how did you come to be interested in the scroll? With a possession such as the cloak of Saint Francis of Assisi, you must have great knowledge of relics—what made you believe the scroll was more than just an antique? I understand that most of the magical commonality view it as nothing more than that."

"Relics are another way for money to buy magical power, and therefore I have a great interest in them. But it was simple deduction that led me to the scroll. Apart from your study of the confluences, and your work at the university, where did you spend the most time? After the dead-end in Tribune, I continued to have your behavior tracked—and I noticed a pattern; India was, for you, a special place. It wasn't situated near any of the powerful confluences that you were most likely to be found; instead, you always came back to India—and more often than not, you came to the Cascabela.

"At first, I thought the scroll was a trinket, a stupid extravagance in collecting, an investment—an antique, as you said. Nowhere in the annals of history is it believed to have had real power—at least nowhere serious. It's a legend, and that's all.

"But then I reviewed all our records of your visits to the Cascabela—and found that through the years, you've consistently taken the scroll from its display for days at a time. Every few years or so. To do what? You wouldn't remove an antique, except to sell it or move it. It might probably be real, I thought.

"What were you doing with it then? Why remove it? To study it? Use its powers? Make a potion, perhaps? I determined to see the scroll for myself, to find out if it held any of the secrets that I so longed to discover. But it was a decoy, a fake—a trap that let you spit in the face of any who would dare try to share in your secret, if there really is one.

"Perhaps your secret is not the scroll at all. I suppose I could have made myself believe in the legends; but it doesn't matter now. To be honest, I doubt that Brevig is the only member of the Preeminent Council who knows something of the Sempiternus. If I had done things differently—hadn't focused so much on you, in proving something to you, in proving you wrong—perhaps I could have continued my pursuit in other directions."

He paused. Eyeing Olivia and me, and seeing the lack of understanding in our faces, he continued with a smile.

"They don't even know Brevig is on the Preeminent Council? These, your friends as you call them, and they know almost nothing about the world of magic that you are such an important part of! Thomas, from afar you were much more intriguing, I must say. Up close, you're not very sharp. How could you not know that?"

"Because like true friends," the professor interrupted, "they move with me in my closest circle, along with my family and loved ones—they don't hover over me, behind me, and in my past, looking for answers and information about me that I'm not ready to share. They know me today, right now, for who I prove myself to be."

Lowen laughed quietly while he eyed us all.

"Well, then. So die the mysteries of Crane and Spindlebrock and the scroll, shared only between us four. And as for you two, who knows if you'll get to keep the secret or if it will be taken from you by your so-called friend! Eternal life is yours, Spindlebrock, while I get quite the other end of the stick, it seems. Your friends will live out their lives and die of old age perhaps, and you will be alone to start it all over, and over, and over again. Names, identities, anything it takes to cover your trail of selfishness."

"I will choose my own fate, Lowen, just as you have done."

"No," Lowen replied. "You have chosen my fate! No one but you."

With this, he pulled a vial from his pocket. In an instant it reached almost to his lips, but Spindlebrock's wand was drawn and the vial ejected from his hands before a drop could touch his tongue. Without hesitating, the professor whipped his wand to the side, spinning the stunned Lowen on the balls of his feet. In a series of motions that took mere moments, he cast a charm that ripped an outlet from the wall behind Lowen, tearing the still-connected thick electrical wire right through the plaster in a cloud of dust and debris, then snapping it from the sparking leads and wrapping it around Lowen tightly. He stood before us bound and secured, with only dizziness as a side-effect.

"You won't die today, not if I can help it. The Council wants me to bring you out to them, and that I shall do. From there, it will be up to them to determine your fate."

"Well," Lowen replied, "perhaps the council would be interested in your secrets as well."

The professor smiled.

"And as for my secrets, you may say what you will about me to the council, Lowen. You will find that they are a tough crowd to surprise, having lived lives as full or more full of secrets than my own."

Lowen—or Crane, however you want to look at it—had basically turned himself in, operating at least in part on the false assumption that his identity had already been revealed to us by Evalyn, who Spindlebrock led him to believe we had captured. And so, the adversary we had pursued for so long had been taken into custody, and with almost no danger to anyone. We walked him out of the casino, where he was received by Tahlia, Leonardo, and three others that I did not recognize; I assumed at the time that these were all on the Preeminent Council, and I was not incorrect. Leonardo was tasked with keeping him secure until a tribunal with the full council could be held, and with all involved agreeing that his business affairs would be delegated to proxies and news of his capture kept private until the council was completed (to protect his reputation in case the council found no fault), the years-long case of W.C. Crane was—at least for the time being—settled.

Chapter 22

A Crinkled Letter

For the benefit of the reader, I omitted almost all of the thoughts and feelings that I experienced during the interview laid out in the last chapter; and I have no intention of detailing them here. As you can plainly see, Crane was the creation of a person obsessed with Professor Spindlebrock, bound and determined to meet an invented specter in every presumed challenge of magical power and capacity. His were the rantings of a frenzied mind, I believe, who glommed on to a person or idea that could receive the concentration of his anger, hate, and whatever else that drove him. He had little to do with me—far less than I had let myself imagine—and so for the moment I'll leave his story where it stands.

Without a doubt, it was an acute mental and emotional strain for both Olivia and me, sitting and listening to everything that I just described, then standing in the parking lot and watching as a small car carried away prisoner the man who had been the cause of so much anxiety and suspense. The strain was multiplied many times over by the weight of the revelations we had so recently absorbed concerning Professor Spindlebrock. But these we bore as people often do in the thick of turbulent and significant events. In our stunned state I think we might have just stood there trapped in our thoughts until the sun went down, had he not spoken.

"Thomas, I can't believe you're not exploding with questions."

"Who says I'm not?"

He turned to us, clearly fighting back emotion.

"I suppose you two have more cause than ever to mistrust me now. Perhaps you feel that I've used you—perhaps I have. I've asked you to trust me many times, and now you see that I haven't trusted you in return. Can we move forward from this?"

Olivia answered. I could see the forgiveness that Sanjay had inspired still shining in her eyes.

"That depends on what happens next. Words won't be enough. You've been living a lie, professor. You have to make that right. For your own sake."

He looked thoughtful, and nodded slowly.

"And what about us, Thomas?"

His tone was imploring, but I hadn't honestly had time to feel anything. Adrenaline was still relentlessly driving my mind and delaying my emotions.

"I don't know what this changes. I guess I'm glad that I know the truth—that we know. But Olivia's right; having a private life is one thing, but all this? It's a lot to process. Things will have to change."

"Karthika would agree with you both; and so do I. But the lies are finally over—it's such relief! You don't know how long I've wanted to get this out of the dark."

"So why didn't you tell us sooner?"

There was challenge in my voice; for some reason, his obvious relief was irritating. I felt none, and I wasn't ready to let him feel any either.

"I was going to tell you. It was going to be on this trip, truly it was."

"Unless something didn't go as planned? When were you going to tell us?"

He pulled a crinkled envelope from his pocket.

"Lowen forced these things out in the open a little sooner than I anticipated—No, Thomas, nothing was going to change my mind. I was going to tell you."

As he spoke, he tore open the letter and scanned through the pages.

"This is a letter I wrote for you two, on the plane from Toronto to New Delhi. Lowen confessed my sins for me; I could have stopped him of course, but it was my intention to reveal all of this to you both very soon anyway, just not at this point. I wasn't ready—I thought it would perhaps be something of a kindness to him, to let him go on the way he did. I guess I thought it might make him feel better to win in that small way at the end. But this letter will prove my original intentions. I was going to give you this after—"

He broke off as he found something in the letter.

"Here we go. Right here—"

Separating a couple pages and stuffing them in his pocket, he folded what remained of the letter and slid it back into the envelope.

"This letter might help. At least, I hope that it will show that I really did mean to tell you about my past, and at the same time give you a more true and accurate accounting of my life than Lowen could have hoped to give. Here, take it. I'll leave you both to read it at your own pace. Come to the front desk when you're ready—I wrote more, but with the way things have gone I think it makes more sense to just show you."

My anger was growing as the adrenaline wore off, but I took the letter and watched stone-faced as Spindlebrock walked away.

* * *

I attempted to summarize the proffered portion of Spindlebrock's letter in an early draft of this volume, but it was suggested by my editor that I simply include it as-is.

Therefore, so that the reader may understand what Olivia and I learned that day, I've included it here:

To my dear friends, Thomas and Olivia:

I'm currently en route to New Delhi, where I trust we'll meet up, to embark on another journey of discovery—an adventure, as some might call it. It may surprise you to learn that I feel a great deal of apprehension in relation to this particular trip, which prompts me to write this letter now. Or, perhaps the element of surprise will have already passed by the time I give you this letter. In any case, my feelings are present, even if my aims are future, so excuse me if I falter.

The fact that you're reading this means that certain facts concerning my life have already been revealed to you. My plan has, for some time, been to tell you everything, but years slip by like a handful of water for me now, and the right time is something even more elusive. However, my writing this means that the time is here, or almost here. I mean to say that I am deciding that the time is right or must be made right, while we're on this trip. So I repeat that if you're reading this, I will have already made certain things about myself clear, most especially the fact that I'm an older man than either of you realized. Some call me a Sempiternus, though I find the term absurd in more ways than one. In my own mind, I'm simply old.

Regardless of terminology, details remain to be shared which I can't imagine sharing in a conversation that would perhaps be filled with too much emotion or shock to adequately and fairly cover everything that I feel should be covered. And therefore, I'm preparing this letter so that I can convey facts on a subject that is, as you can hopefully understand, very difficult to broach.

As with anything, it is probably best if I start from the beginning. In the year eighteen eighteen my father was stationed in Madras (modern day Chennai). It was a few years after the Vellore fort mutiny, and the British were building up their forces there. He brought with him his young wife, my mother, who unknown to either of them was pregnant with their first child. I was born in the year eighteen nineteen, and named Cyrus Cardamom Spindlebrock.

My mother's health suffered in the foreign climate, and as a result she spent a great deal of time traveling to Britain and elsewhere for care. I was brought up primarily by servants who were all part of the local magical commonality, my parents both being magicians. By the age of four, it was clear that my innate magical abilities were prodigious, and as a result my formal magical education started very early. Because of my situation I was not only educated in what my parents referred to as "orthodox magic", but also in a very eastern magical tradition, provided by the best magicians that could be had in that area—or brought in for a price that my family could afford.

At the age of six, magicians from around the world had begun to visit on their own, as word of my abilities spread. I was already being courted for training in the best schools, and with the brightest researchers in a variety of fields. But I was too young—my father decided to pause my education in magic, until I was old enough for it to be something I chose to pursue, rather than something that engulfed my life. The visits stopped, and the flame of excitement around my name completely died out.

However, my fascination with magic continued, and I carried on my pursuits with the help of the Indian magicians that were charged with my care. My parents both knew of my activities and approved of them—they allowed me to delve into magic without the spotlight that they feared would cause me so much grief. It was at this time that I first met Sanjay and Karthika, the two magicians that most shaped who I am as a person. If circumstances have not allowed me to introduce you both to them before you read this, then I promise to make that happen very soon.

I should probably clarify—the Sanjay and Karthika of today are not what one might call Sempiternus. According to their beliefs, they are the reincarnations of two teachers that I knew as a child. Whether anyone else believes this or not is irrelevant—I myself claim no knowledge one way or the other on the matter; they are my friends, and that suffices.

One of my first magical obsessions had to do with magic relating to health, vitality, and the life force. This was when I was about twelve years old and my mother's health began to fail. Health is, unsurprisingly, one of the oldest areas of study known to man or magician, as the extension of life has always been of interest to mortal beings who so universally face the uncertainties of death. In India, I found a wealth of information, both real and contrived, on the subject.

My mother died when I was sixteen years old, and for the next two years I covered intense feelings of guilt and depression with travel and research—still primarily on the extension of life, but also on interactions with those who have passed on: Ghosts. Olivia and Thomas, when you said that you were both interested in this area of study, I was excited and apprehensive. Can you see how this subject appealed to me—the thought of communicating with those who have passed on? I've considered and studied it now for nearly two hundred years.

At age eighteen, I returned to India. My father was now a lieutenant general, with significant influence. His superior, the general, was also a magician—and he and my father presumed to encourage a connection between their children. However, the general's daughter—named Ella —had already made a connection with a young officer in the Indian army. I supported them, and when their fathers thought I was spending time with her, she was actually spending time with the Indian officer that she already loved.

After a few months, another officer under the general's command became suspicious, and sent soldiers to spy on our meetings. The young Indian officer was discovered, fled, and was never seen again. Ella was devastated, and I was her only friend through that difficult time. Some years later, we married; she was lost at sea on a research expedition about one year after our wedding. These events were some of the most painful of my life.

By about eighteen seventy, I had discovered that multiple methods existed for extending life; and I realized that if I were going to extend my own life (I had reasons to, at this point, which I will get to toward the end of this letter) I would have to do so clandestinely. Working toward this end, I first abandoned all kinship and friendship, and became a recluse. While developing this reclusive persona, I worked tirelessly to destroy or depersonalize as many traces of my impact on the magical commonality as I could; my research, my publications, and even the memories of the people I had worked with, were altered or destroyed.

As I faded or forced my way into obscurity, I began an experiment which consisted of a new and false identity—that of a young magician named Charles Morgan. Using potions and other magic to alter my appearance, I gave this false identity enough substance to be accepted as real—and then the nobody who was Charles Morgan, to the shock of all, became the apprentice to the now-reclusive but still venerated Cyrus Spindlebrock.

As Morgan I accomplished very little, by design, and Spindlebrock continued to languish in the public eye. The two eventually fell together into obscurity and irrelevance. The sole benefit and goal of this entire charade was accomplished: I could now move about it the world as Charles Morgan, instead of Cyrus Spindlebrock. You see, I couldn't very well remain Cyrus forever; he had to age and die and be forgotten, as far as everyone else viewed things.

Now that I think about it, I suppose that neither of you is very familiar with the traditions surrounding magical apprenticeship. One thing you need to understand is that in general, this sort of relationship only exists when a magician is either extremely powerful, or extremely wealthy. As Spindlebrock I was both, but in the eyes of the world only my wealth passed to Morgan.

This process of transforming from Spindlebrock to Morgan was effective, and so I continued to use it. My wealth was the subject of the apprenticeship between Charles Morgan and my next identity, Tobias Andrews. This false identity carried me from about the year nineteen hundred to just before World War II, when Marius Robles came about. The Great Depression and the war had impacted many, but Robles had come out greater, richer, and more well-known. The fortune of Marius Robles —my fortune—had grown to legendary extremes, and could no longer be the fortune of a recluse. I had likewise continued to grow in magical knowledge and power, quite in secret— and had tired of the restrictions of his protective

*identity that consisted of a rich but
unaccomplished magician.*

*As Robles aged in the eyes of the world, a new
apprentice identity was needed. In about
nineteen seventy, Lucas Brevig was created.
This alter-ego will be familiar to you both, of
course. Lucas Brevig was designed to be less of a
recluse, more involved in the commonality. He
revealed himself as a magician not only of
wealth, but of peculiar talent; the world saw it
as talent, which is to be expected when you're
evaluating one who has lived almost two
hundred years, without knowing that key fact.
So great was Brevig's apparent talent that he
quickly rose through the ranks of the magical
commonality, surpassing all but a very select
few—those few who were in several ways his
equals. In time, Brevig took his place among the
ranks of the Preeminent Council.*

*It feels very odd to write about myself in the
third-person, but I almost feel like when I look
at my life, I'm looking at the lives of others. I
lost myself in these identities for a long time, but
as Lucas Brevig I began to see myself, my life, as
something new. I imagine that it's confusing to
read all at once like this, but I thought that the
core facts would be the easiest to understand.*

*My position and activities in the Preeminent
Council were not what I thought they would be,
and a few short years after I became Lucas
Brevig—in nineteen seventy three to be precise
—Cyrus Cardamom Spindlebrock was re-
introduced to the world once more, as an
aspiring magician, the new apprentice to Lucas*

*Brevig. In all those years of obscurity, I had
never showed myself to another without the use
of a collection of transformative charms and
potions; but now, I was finally resuming my
original identity, and with it my real
appearance—with a new idea of what my
purpose might become. For years, I carried on
the facade of being Brevig and Spindlebrock,
both of which were seen and known in society
(though never together), until about the year
two thousand two, when Brevig started down
the path of reclusiveness, leaving Spindlebrock
to manage most of his public-facing affairs.*

*This catches you up, at least at a high level, with
who I am and who I have been these many
years. However, these bare facts don't really
explain why I did what I did, and what I hoped
to gain or achieve through my efforts. To
understand that, you must understand why
your interest in ghosts and your willingness to
pursue things in India was so meaningful to
me. The events that are likely to unfold when
we all arrive there are what have caused me to
write this letter; they are the impetus for my
revealing these things to you at this time. I
believe in Providence, as you both ought to
know by now—but I won't bother you with my
beliefs.*

*The Cascabela is a place of deep meaning for
me, a place that ties in with my—*

At this point, the letter broke off, the remaining pages
having been withheld. The information we did have was
mind bending to a degree—but as the professor had never

revealed much of his past to either of us, the fact that so much had been hidden was not the most shocking part. That we were friends with a magician who was at the time nearly two hundred years old—that was difficult to wrap our heads around.

We read and re-read the letter, and talked about some of the things we found there. It did provide answers and insights, but we still wondered about the scroll, the confluences, Karthika, the auction, Sanjay; in short, everything we had encountered on our trip. Anxious to learn more, and somewhat calmed, we reconnected with Spindlebrock.

Chapter 23

Real Answers

Spindlebrock was waiting for us at the front desk when we arrived. He looked both apprehensive and relieved at our arrival. He signaled for us to follow him.

"I promised you several times that we would have the opportunity to pursue the very thing that you came to India for," he told us as we made our way through the gaming hall.

"Well, I think we're past all that at this point—there will be more opportunities in the future, but it seems so irrelevant just now."

"I thought you might feel that way, Olivia. Thomas, I suppose you feel the same way?"

"Sort of," I admitted. "I guess it seems like ghosts aren't what we thought they were."

"Precisely true—and at the same time, entirely false. To say that ghosts, or the various manifestations that people call ghosts, aren't always what you thought, would be more accurate. You've seen me as a ghostlike form, and yet you know that there was a scientific explanation for it; even if the science is slightly beyond your understanding at this juncture."

We both admitted that he was right.

"Then how would you explain Daksh? You both saw him. You both know that he has been haunting this place for quite some time."

We looked at one another, but had no answer.

"I'm going to open the mystery of Daksh to you, and answer some questions about the scroll at the same time. Then we'll delve a little further on the issue of ghosts."

We were heading into the vaults. He was silent until we reached the center.

"Here we are, at the inner chamber. I've arranged for a work crew as you can see. And, I've had all of my display's security measures disabled."

About a dozen men were standing around, several with ladders.

"Please," the professor commanded loudly, "remove the top of the display!"

At his word ladders were placed, and in no time the brass top was off. He commanded the glass be removed, and it was done. He then dismissed the workers, and after a few words with the security staff, the entire series of vaults was emptied of anyone save the professor, Olivia, and me.

"Thomas, you kept the scroll at the close of the auction, you'll recall. I took it from you when we changed you back into your clothes—while you were passed out, after touching Evalyn. Here is the scroll."

He produced the scroll we had seen at the auction.

"It has been called a fake several times recently, by many including myself. That is in fact true, and it is one way to look at things; a more accurate term could be duplicate, or replica. It is fake in that it is not the original, but it is also an exact copy. And by exact, I mean in the same way that the stone in your pocket is an exact copy of another stone, Olivia. In short, it is a version or iteration of the same item, shifted only very slightly in phase to a higher or lower plane —please, don't ask me to delve deeper, those are questions for Sanjay."

I'm not sure about Olivia, but I was feeling almost entirely lost, and couldn't have formed a useful question if I wanted to.

"Now, Olivia, I want you to remove the red velvet around the base of the scroll case. There, now observe the base itself. Do you see the markings?"

"Yes, it's like an ultra-precise ruler was etched into the brass."

"It was. Take a look Thomas, I know you'll find this interesting too."

I did, and noticed that the scroll case had been placed with extreme precision, right in the middle of the base. I shared my observation aloud.

"That's right," the professor continued. "And if you would have been here when this vault was built, you would have noted that the foundation, walls, and the entire design and execution were carried out with equal precision, all to allow this case to be placed in this exact location. I know, because I was there. I designed and oversaw the building of this museum."

I shuddered at his words. For some reason, the realities of his long life hadn't quite solidified in my mind; every fresh allusion to them was startling.

"I wasn't upset about the loss of the replica scroll merely because it was an exact copy—you see, the words and runes cannot be used on their own. A photo of the scroll doesn't give you the scroll or its power, for example; you have to have the real, actual, original scroll. I was concerned because the replica is the key to obtaining the original. I knew this, and it could only be a matter of time—be it years or centuries—before someone else learned the fact."

As he spoke, he carefully replaced the replica scroll in the scroll case, rotated the discs to a specific order, then closed and locked the lid.

"The scroll case is a Selectivam Ostium of sorts. It is bound to an identical case, located in a tiny cylindrical chamber sealed in the foundation of the vault. A unique spell causes the scrolls to change places—or travel between the two realities of the Selectivam Ostium, if you will—thus allowing one to obtain the original scroll here in the museum."

"Amazing!" I blurted out. "So, the real scroll was kept safe, buried in concrete in a tiny space that no one knew about or could access. If they tried to steal it—as they did!– then they'd only get a useless copy. I wondered why you would have trusted the security measures here, which while sufficient for many things, seemed inadequate for something so rare—now I know, you weren't trusting the modern security measures, really, you were trusting this clever setup! And this museum—it must be built on a confluence?"

Spindlebrock smiled. Looking back now, I think he was pleased that our relationship was still one where I was likely to interrupt him at any moment with my enthusiasm. After confessing such a profound lie as he had, I certainly understand the kind of relief that must have been growing in his heart.

"Yes, that's all exactly right," he answered. "And yet, even the replica was a terrible risk. But I could think of no other way to secure it. Such an object can never truly be safe; of such a powerful relic, discovery and theft are eventualities that can't be avoided, only delayed. This system was a delay, and it has served me well all these years. By keeping the scroll out in public—or, so everyone thought—I was tacitly admitting that the scroll had no real power. Who would leave it lying about, even guarded, if it did? While on the other hand if I had hidden it, as so many have tried over the years, that would have led to the same ends that have always accompanied the scroll: treachery, betrayal, and death."

He paused, examining the scroll case. He seemed intent on something, as if he were fighting against his own will perhaps.

"I wanted the scroll, long ago. I wanted the power it promised. But that was before I knew what it was. Then I made a mistake, and I wanted the scroll and its power for a different reason—I wanted to fix my mistake. I thought that I could do some good, that I could change things. But I've found that one person taking that much power—"

He broke off for a moment, choked with emotion.

"It never ends well."

He cleared his throat, and breathed in deeply.

"Now, this spell is like several you've heard recently; in the temple, traveling through the confluences—but it is a little different. However, there will be no need to memorize it, because this is the last time that it will ever be used."

He performed the spell quietly. When he was done, he rotated the discs and opened the case. From it, he withdrew a scroll that looked exactly like the one he had put in. He turned it over in his hands, then put it in his jacket pocket.

"Come," he said, "I'll show you now what the scroll has to do with Daksh."

As we exited the vaults, he explained out next destination.

"Olivia, this next spot will probably interest you more than it will Thomas. You recall, Thomas, that there is no basement under the vaults. The same is true for most of the casino; but in the oldest part of the building—the original part that was here before the rest—there is a small basement that few know about. The original building was a sort of a temple, not entirely unlike the ones that you usually see in Tamil Nadu, apart from the architecture. But, it was here before all of those, and it was built here because of the confluence. I know this because as a boy, Sanjay brought me here to train."

By this time we had reached a very plain looking locked door in that older part of the casino which I've mentioned. Spindlebrock had the key; the door opened to reveal a dark stairwell. A cool, humid, earthy breeze blew past us as we stood peering into the darkness.

"It's dark, but I believe you both have flashlights on your phones."

We did, and we illuminated them as we made our way down the wooden stairs. They terminated at a hard dirt floor.

"It's not level," the professor warned. "In fact, you'll notice that it's very much a sort of dip; it was an old riverbed, a portion of the one I showed you from the mountain peak, Thomas."

As we scanned around in the dark, our lights rested on an object several yards away.

"Olivia, this will look very familiar."

She advanced on her own into the black.

"It's a kattumaram, just like the one that Sanjay used to train me," she said as she approached the object. "It has the same markings. Professor, you didn't tell me that you had any elemental abilities."

"I don't, really, only what little can be gained through heavy training and study. As a child, I was exposed to any and every magical discipline, and I thought back then that I could master them all. It took many years for me to accept that such a person cannot be made—we must necessarily have weaknesses."

"But, what's this got to do with Daksh?" Olivia queried.

"Well, I told you the story of Daksh in my office at the university before we left Canada—how he fell in love with a young woman he could not marry. I also told you that my father tried to arrange something between myself and a young woman who was already in love with someone else; that someone else was Daksh."

Olivia gasped.

"You mean, you helped them—but you said the young man ran away and was never seen again?"

"They had been discovered, and the girl's father was going to have the young man court-martialed. I feared for his life and we fled here with soldiers in pursuit. I knew the spell to shift this kattumaram through time; this setup is something that Sanjay uses to increase elemental focus. In my arrogance, I thought that I could bring him with me, leave him there until trouble was gone, and bring him back later. Sanjay warned me, but—"

"You mean in the middle of the spell, he got off the kattumaram?" she asked.

"I told him to, and he did. He trusted me, and I trapped him in-between time, in the Strata Temporis."

We stood quietly, waiting for the professor to continue.

"It was the first of many mistakes. I thought I could make it right. The idea of dying myself, and leaving him trapped—what if there was an afterlife? How could I die and go there in peace, knowing he could never reach it? He would live forever, trapped outside of anything we would call a life."

"Professor," I interrupted. "Didn't you say that you married the girl, the one—"

I didn't quite know how to finish the question without potentially causing pain.

"Yes, I did. Her name was Ella Louise May. It's a longer and more personal story than I'm willing to share—but yes, we married. I think she was willing to view the whole thing as an accident, and put it in the past. But I was not. I wanted to fix it. She helped me; until she passed away on a research trip that had in view that very aim. I couldn't forgive myself, no matter how I tried. Perhaps she would not have died, maybe that trip would never have happened, if I hadn't done what I had done? It haunted me, and after that I pursued the scroll to buy more time.

"How long can pride lead a person down winding paths of compromise? For me it was lifetimes. I relied on myself and myself alone, no matter the cost. Trapped in my own personal hell, in a sense. Until I met you and Thomas, I thought I would never be able to stop trying on my own to make it right. I thought I would never be free."

"What do you mean?" I asked.

"I met Olivia, and I thought that with her talents I might be able to find some new way to get him out. That is to say, I thought that perhaps she could excel where I was inadequate; the first step away from pride, I think, is understanding that you can't do everything on your own. I saw in her something bigger than myself, something more than I could ever accomplish. But my hope was thin; even Sanjay, who is exceptionally gifted, had never been able to help me.

"Then I met you, Thomas—or, you met me, more accurately. And with your gift, new ideas started presenting themselves to my mind. My research efforts were redoubled, I was connecting ideas that had never been connected in the history of magic, that I could discover. I made a breakthrough in elemental research just before the scroll was stolen, one that I thought might give me a chance —give us a chance.

"When it became clear that we would need to attend the Glebovich auction, everything fell into place; destiny or Providence brought us to that point. It was an opportunity to test my breakthrough theory. I already explained that through the Signum Dominii—an object bound to me— Olivia was able not only to bring me into a phase of time that I was not a part of, she was able to bring me out of it again. And this with only a few days training. With such a powerful gift, she and I could exchange the object that she brought with her, and she could match our phases. Of course, I hadn't realized that without physically seeing me, she'd run into trouble. What you two discovered with Conexus, that was more than just a breakthrough; it was an earth-shattering revelation."

"So that's why you were willing to take the risk. You wanted to test your theory on yourself, to see if it would work."

"That's right, Olivia. And I thank you again for that—there was no danger to you, I assure you. To me, it was worth any risk to either solve the problem, or be done with trying."

I stopped them both.

"Wait—you didn't both hold the actual Signum Dominii though, right? She made a copy of it, and passed you that. Isn't that what happened? I thought you said a copy didn't have any power, just like the scroll?"

"We're not talking about magical power, as with relics. The copy of the Signum Dominii would not have worked to get into the auction, for example—it would have failed the counter spell. No, we're talking about a power that binds certain objects to their creators, something more or something deeper than magic. When you took the replica scroll, you felt that it was mine, right?"

"I did."

"And yet, that replica or copy was created by Sanjay, not by me—no, I shouldn't say it that way; he didn't create anything. What he did was focus his energy to shift the scroll's state and fragment it, making two versions of it appear—like I already said, Sanjay could explain it more clearly. The point is, both the original and the copy are linked to me."

"The original is linked to you, then? The Rognvald Scroll? How?" Olivia asked.

"It is. You see, when I finally obtained the scroll, I realized that the work of its discoveries was only partially completed. I finished that work—and the process of that work connected that scroll to me deeply. In point of fact, I am the creator of the completed scroll, the finisher."

He stopped. The earth seemed to sigh, I thought, and I felt its breath once again as I did when we first entered the basement.

"They don't use this space for anything," the professor continued. "Like the tables, the kattumaram is trapped in time. It can't be destroyed; not easily. And so, the temple was built around it, and the casino around that—and here it has stayed. I've visited it many times, to test different theories. And here we are now. Knowing what you know about my life, would you consent to help me try to bring Daksh out? I think we could do it, together."

I can't speak for what Olivia experienced in that moment, but for me it was a rush of empathy and a willingness to embrace the hope that seemed to be filling my old friend. Neither of us hesitated to answer that we absolutely would absolutely be willing to help. He looked at us a long time before he could speak. He thanked us, but struggled again with his emotions before he could continue.

"We will come back to this place—but first, we need to meet Karthika and Sanjay. They each have something that we're going to need."

Chapter 24

Daksh Parikh

When he said that we were going to meet Karthika and Sanjay, I thought that meant we'd be spending the remainder of the afternoon and evening driving to pick them up, or waiting for them to arrive; but to my surprise, we heard Karthika's voice as soon as we returned to the lobby. Apparently, she and Sanjay had been sent for when we were on our way back from Belarus. Spindlebrock had anticipated and planned for the events that he had so long hoped for.

She greeted us warmly, embracing us each in turn. That look that Spindlebrock so easily discerns in my face—of questions burning—was readily apparent to me in hers. But she asked nothing, she only noted that Sanjay had taken a walk in the woods beyond the pools. The professor proposed that we all go together to find him, and so we did.

In my mind, I had guessed that we would find him toward the end of the trail, near where we had seen Daksh, and that's precisely where he was. He had climbed off the trail, and was standing in the riverbed, just as Olivia and I had done.

He was a small man, hunched over with age. His white kuta went well past the knees, and he had a neatly tucked white turban. He spoke in perfect English, and his voice was as clear as crystal.

"I think he must come here often. This flowed right under the old temple grounds, and there is power in the path of water. It would be easiest for him to walk here, up and down the river."

We all watched as he gently tapped the rocks with his feet, but no one said a thing.

"The first trick was always finding him. We couldn't try anything unless we could find him, and the more time went by the harder he has become to find. I think, maybe, he spends very little time in there now. When was he last seen?"

Olivia answered.

"Thomas and I saw him here in this very spot, a few days ago."

"That is good. Did he say anything?"

"He asked if it was time to try again."

"Perhaps he will be nearby. We can try—but Cyrus, you know that last time he was gone for years."

"I think," began the professor, "that over time, he has drifted slightly out of his original phase cycle, so that we cross his path less and less. But we're not going to wait for him this time. I have a theory that Thomas and Olivia can help bring him to us."

The old guru lifted his eyes to mine. They sparkled like his voice.

"That is very good. And what do you think, Thomas? Is this something you can do?"

The professor often has faith in me accomplishing things that he hasn't even explained to me yet. But he's a smart man, and I trusted that he knew what he was talking about.

"If the professor believes it's possible, then it's worth trying," I answered.

He smiled, and patted me on the arm.

"And Olivia, what does the professor think you can do?"

"I'm not sure what he thinks I can do that you cannot, Sanjay."

The man turned to Spindlebrock, who spoke.

"It's impossible to insult you, my old friend. You know as well as I do that someone with a gift like Olivia doesn't come along every generation—she doesn't know how rare her gift is, or how natural it comes for her, compared to others. It's not that I don't think you could do it, of course—it's that I want her to do it. Besides, she's already done it once, with Thomas' help, so I know she can do it again."

It was Spindlebrock's turn to smile now. Sanjay chuckled.

"Very good, Cyrus, you have my attention. What is this story you tell? What has she already done?"

He related an abbreviated version of the events in Belarus.

"This is very encouraging! Well, I think that we have all that we need—do we truly have all that we need, Cyrus?"

"I believe so."

"Ah, but there is a problem."

We all looked at him, but no one spoke.

"Yes, there is a real problem. Karthika does not have all that she needs."

We turned to her. She looked confused.

"She spends a lot of time working and studying in that cave," he continued. "And now she finds herself at a resort of luxury. She has not had dinner, she has not relaxed! How can we continue when she is in need this way? Can we not look to her needs, and all our needs, so that we can be comfortable and relaxed when we begin? Is this not wisdom, Cyrus?"

"It most certainly is. Come, let me show you all a wonderful spot."

Spindlebrock led us all to a most beautiful sitting area arranged with a view of the sunset, where we ordered food and drink, and enjoyed one another's company. We ate and talked and relaxed until the stars were out, when Karthika recommended we move forward. Then we made our way to the basement, this time with a lantern that Spindlebrock had procured. As we approached the kattumaram, the professor shared his plan.

"The boat is narrow, but it's long enough to hold four of us and Daksh. Sanjay, you'll stand by and place your hands on the boat while you read the carvings, and steady our movement through time; I will do the same from within the Strata Temporis. Olivia, you'll sit in the very front but facing backward toward Thomas, who will sit here. I'll sit behind Thomas, with Karthika behind me. Mother, do you have the pendant?"

She procured a black-patinated silver pendant, large and round, carved intricately with a scene that resembled a garden.

"Daksh made this as a gift for Ella, who in turn gave it to me. Karthika has kept it for me all these years. I'd like you to hold it for a few moments, Thomas. There's no need to tell us what you find, unless you wish to or need to."

He handed it to me. Instinctively, I closed my eyes to focus. I felt the presence, personality, and emotion of Daksh Parikh, but none of them clearly. It was as if he were fading in and out of existence, alive in moments and gone in others. When I could sense him, a hollow despondency pervaded my mind; in his present state and experience, he truly believed he had nothing to live for. I opened my eyes and gave the pendant back.

"Thomas, once we're all in our places, you'll hold this in your open palm as you face Olivia, who will be holding your wrist. Sanjay, you will begin, and Olivia knows what to do for her part of the charm—and we four will be transported into the strata. Sanjay uses a stone during training; Olivia, you will use the pendant to match us with Daksh's time, and Thomas will help draw you and Daksh together. That's the theory at least. Do you each understand your part?"

We confirmed that we did. Spindlebrock motioned for us to take our places, and we began to situate ourselves.

He turned to Karthika.

"Mother, I asked you here for several reasons. The pendant you could have easily sent along with Sanjay, but I sincerely wanted you to be here to witness this. Also, we need your powers to help ensure our safety; with your telekinetic abilities, I want you to make sure that none of us leaves the kattumaram—no matter what. I hardly trust myself to stay put, I'm so overwhelmed with what is about to happen. And I want there to be no risk to any of us, in this attempt. I don't want to make things worse."

He paused, and Karthika stroked his arm. She assured him that no one would leave the kattumaram. Spindlebrock helped her onto the boat, then climbed on himself.

"Again, thank you—all of you. I've held and lost so many hopes over the years; I'm cherishing them all now. But even if this doesn't work, I want you to know that the fact that I have four people who are willing to help me as you have means more than you may ever know."

The charm was carried out exactly as Spindlebrock instructed, and the experience was in some ways similar to the one that Olivia described in her narrative, earlier in this volume. We commenced in a dark, empty basement space, a dirt expanse that was host to nothing but a gentle depression and an ancient wooden boat. Unlike Olivia's experience, our riverbed did not fill with water; but the basement roof, and all of the building above us, dissipated almost instantly, exposing us to the expansive night sky. Rocks, wood debris, and low plants crowded around us, almost piling one on top of the other, until it felt like we were in the middle of a primitive jungle. The spot where the kattumaram was placed, long before any structure was built there, was near the edge of a small precipice, just beyond the tree line.

I felt Daksh more strongly now, and somehow I imagined that he felt my presence as well. Sanjay had grown light, then transparent, and now invisible—yet we could still hear the steady cadence of his voice. As I took this all in, I noticed that Olivia was focused intently on the pendant. I focused on it as well, reading his heart, experiencing his fears, disappointments, and countless years of trapped emptiness. These I fought through, desperate to delve for something better in his past, buried perhaps deep in his psyche; and I eventually found Ella. Not her, but the memory of her from his perspective. His hopes, his love, his dreams. As I did, I saw a faint light coming down the dry riverbed—it was Daksh, transparent and glowing gently.

He made his way to us quietly, almost apprehensively I thought. Perhaps it was the sight of Spindlebrock, but something seemed to give him a sudden confidence; he approached.

"We've never tried with so many helpers at once. Cyrus, what do you want me to do."

Whether Spindlebrock was petrified and silenced from the suspense of the moment, or something else, I did not know. Perhaps it was that same paralysis that I had experienced when I saw the professor walk through the castle gate. Or, perhaps lifetimes of anticipation were taking their toll all at once. But it didn't matter, because without hesitation Olivia paused her incantation and answered the young man.

"Come, watch the pendant Daksh, watch it closely!"

He approached us with curiosity. The pendant seemed almost foreign to his eye, I thought. But he reached out and touched it. One finger, then two. His ghostly form seemed to flicker.

"Focus, Olivia!"

It was the voice of Sanjay.

"Tell him to sit on the kattumaram, hurry!"

He could not hear Sanjay, but Olivia relayed his instructions and his urgency. Daksh obeyed; still touching the pendant, he sat on the front of the boat, just behind Olivia. She began her incantation again, her eyes now firmly closed.

A copy of his pendant began to rise out of the original. There was no patina; it shone as freshly polished silver. Without a word, Olivia took the pendant and thrust it into Daksh's hands. In that instant the spell was broken, and we found ourselves once again in the ancient basement of the Cascabela.

"What is this? Where am I?"

Daksh shouted in his clear British accent, leaping from the boat and then crouching and scanning all around him for danger. For a moment, no person or object in his surroundings was familiar; then he recognized the kattumaram he had just abandoned.

"That boat, but where's—"

His eyes rested on Spindlebrock.

"Cyrus?"

The professor got off the boat and stood, tears streaming down his face. The rest of us followed.

"I'm sorry, Daksh. I'm so sorry."

The young man was confused.

"You're old. Why are you old, Cyrus, what's going on? Is this a disguise to hide from the soldiers?"

He pawed at his own face, as if maybe he would find a similar mask of age.

"It's no disguise. I made a mistake."

Comprehension dawned on his young face. He looked at the silver pendant in his hands.

"Ella! Where is she?"

Spindlebrock's mouth opened and shut, but nothing came out. He looked at me, appealing for help, but I didn't know what to say. Karthika finally spoke.

"She's not here, Daksh. Please, let us leave this place and we will explain everything."

"No, they're after me! Cyrus, tell them!

"We're safe now," he replied, his voice cracking. "We're safe. No one is coming. They're gone—they're all gone."

Chapter 25

Unfinished Business

It was several days before things settled. Spindlebrock, Sanjay, and Karthika all left the Cascabela with Daksh that night, to take him somewhere safe and comfortable, where he could be told all that he needed to be told. Each of them was a part of his story, and they alone could hope to answer his questions; knowing that we couldn't make things any easier for him, Olivia and I decided to stay behind.

After they had gone, we were informed that the professor had left a credit card at the front desk, with a note telling us to make the most of it. After some discussion, we decided to get some space from everything; we checked out of the Cascabela the following morning, found a nice hotel in Salem, and for a few days we explored the city as wealthy tourists might.

The professor eventually found our hotel (or more likely he always knew where we had gone), and surprised us one morning with a message. It read, "When you're ready, tell the front desk. A driver will be called, who will bring you to the temple." It was signed, "C.C."

We had no plans for that day, and were anxious to hear more about how everything stood—and to eventually get back home to Toronto—so we told the clerk that we would be ready as soon as our bags were packed. By the time we had cleared out our rooms, the promised car was waiting. After a familiar but still circuitous drive, we arrived at the temple. Spindlebrock was standing outside, and greeted us each with an uncustomary hug.

"I didn't want you to have to sneak in like we did last time, when I thought that perhaps we were being followed. Plus, I wasn't sure if you would have thought to bring bananas."

He guided us through a back entrance, to the door that leads to the underground chamber.

"I want you to try to open it on your own—go ahead."

Neither of us had had an opportunity to recall or practice the spell, but I had made some notes about it; using these, and with some prompting from Spindlebrock where my notes were deficient or incorrect, I was eventually able to open the door.

"Wonderful! Update those notes—and remind me at some point to tell you the location of this temple; it's a little hard to find at first."

We passed through the Selectivam Ostium and into the tunnel. The stone was already slid out of place to let us enter. Karthika closed it once we were all inside. She rushed up to Olivia and greeted her with a kiss on the check, then greeted me no less warmly. I motioned questioningly toward Daksh, who was sitting on a couch facing away from us. She cast a furtive glance at Spindlebrock, then led us over to join him.

"Daksh," she said quietly as we approached, "we have visitors."

He nodded. I couldn't quite make out his expression; he was exhausted and wan, but not pained I thought.

"Thank you. Welcome, my name is Daksh."

"I'm Olivia."

"And I'm Thomas Martin. It's good to finally speak with you, Daksh."

He smiled briefly.

"Cyrus has told me much about you two. I'm very grateful to you."

"It was nothing," Olivia chimed in.

"Well, it sounded like a lot more than nothing. It sounded like you were the only ones that could help in— how many years was it again Cyrus?"

"Over a hundred and eighty years."

He raised his eyebrows and nodded.

"Do you remember anything? From while you were trapped, I mean," I asked.

"Not a thing. Sanjay said I would start to remember, but I didn't want to. Cyrus is apparently an even better magician now than he was—he had a potion made for me. I will never remember that time now, I think."

There was silence as this sank in.

"What will you do?" asked Olivia.

"Cyrus said I could come back with you all to the Province of Quebec—which is now Candanda—"

"Canada," the professor corrected.

"Yes, Canada. He said I could go to school there. But I can't. What I mean is that I'm a military man, and an Indian. I learned that India is now a liberated country; I don't think I would be of any use to the military at this point, but I want to get to know my home again—and I don't think I could feel comfortable somewhere else, with everything so different now."

He looked down at the modern clothing that he was wearing, and then at the computers.

"These machines—it's amazing that non-magical people have finally embraced some form of magic at least."

"There's so much more than that—it must be overwhelming," observed Olivia.

298

Daksh only nodded.

"So I will stay with Sanjay, and learn my place in this new world."

"I think it's a perfect plan," added Spindlebrock." You'll find that this new world is full of opportunities of every kind. And as I've shown you, we can communicate instantly, anywhere on the planet."

"Even in space among the stars, apparently. I can't believe that."

"Yes, even in space. But you can study all of that, and learn it in your own time and way. Sanjay is a very capable teacher, and will know how to ease you into it all. And I've setup a fund for you—"

"I would prefer to work."

"Daksh, you may work if you choose—I only want you to understand that you will never lack for anything you need— ever."

The young man only nodded.

"Now, there's a reason we're all together here today, and it's not just to talk about how the world has changed. There's one unfinished piece of business that I need to address."

From his pocket, he withdrew the scroll. He removed the leather straps, and unrolled it.

"The Spindlebrock Scroll—no, it just doesn't have that ring to it. The Rognvald Scroll!"

He held it up for us to examine. Then, to our surprise, he passed it around.

"Rognvald wished to cement those in his bloodline as powerful rulers, so the legends goes. It was popularly believed that he meant for this scroll to ensure that they would have power forever; the Kingmaker scroll, it has been called. But as you know, this scroll isn't about power at all, it's about extending life.

"You see, Rognvald already had power through his well-positioned family and friends, and that kind of power isn't terribly hard to keep if you're wise. What he couldn't control was his descendants. He understood that foolishness and selfishness would eventually destroy their position, because he understood history and human nature. So he decided that he would focus on living forever, rather than entrusting his dreams to others, even his own progeny.

"Scientific knowledge in his day was extremely limited— and make no mistake, he was a scientist. It was a stroke of luck that led him to postulate that something in the body must break as time passed, and then to seek to repair that something. He didn't even have a term for it, he called it only the 'essence of life,' as was common in his day among magicians.

"He did not find a way to repair it. So, he started looking for ways to replace it. His research took a dark turn at that point—he sought to steal life from others, and process it into a form that he could use for himself. It is unpleasant to report that he did have some success in his research; his methods were crude and his magic rudimentary, but he actually found a way to do what he intended. He became a murderer and a tyrant, lost the trust of his people, and produced a literal swarm of enemies. In the end, the cost of his success and tyranny was infamy. He lost the very thing that he longed to keep, when he paid for his misdeeds with his life—and justly so. But, his scroll survived."

He retrieved the scroll from us and rolled it up again, carefully replacing the leather straps.

"I told you that I completed his work, and perhaps you're wondering how. I will tell you this: I never murdered anyone. By the time I obtained the scroll, science was far enough along that I could take his research and convert it to animal studies. Today, such a thing would perhaps sound almost as hideous as murder to some people, but in the eighteen hundreds that wasn't really a consideration.

"What I found was, I could take certain portions of genetic material from one subject, and transfer them to another subject. I could extend a lab mouse's life from the average one year, to a maximum tested lifespan of over a decade—ten lifetimes, with no side effects. In fact, quite the opposite; I found that the mice whose lives I extended were healthier, less prone to disease, and quicker to heal from injury, compared to the control subjects.

"The problem was, when I took genetic material from one mouse—I did this with magic spells, mind you, not with needles and scalpels or some other crude mechanical method—the mouse that lost the material aged faster. I was literally stealing time from one mouse, and giving it to another."

He paused, and set the scroll down on the small round table in front of us.

"There is no excuse for what I did—not to the mice, but to people, I mean to say. I finished the scroll, and used it to siphon years of life away from countless people. Small amounts here and there, but time nevertheless. I justified myself, that I was doing important work, that I was trying to help, to save, to progress humanity even! Anything to make myself feel better. But you cannot feel right when you are doing wrong.

"The upside of my mistakes was this: they forced me to examine myself. Misery, theft—sin, if I can call it that without confusing any of you—these were all overcome as I learned more, and explored things that I hadn't before considered. But I never overcame my desire to fix the mistake I made with you, Daksh; and so, I prolonged reform. I'm sorry to have to confess it, but it is true.

"Karthika has been chiding me for decades to destroy the scroll, and to move on with my life—my lives, as she states things. Now that you are safe, Daksh, I can finally do that. I'm sorry, Karthika, that I was not strong enough to do it sooner. But I want you all to witness here and now that my resolve is real."

His wand was out, and pointed at the scroll. No one said a word as he began the first spell. He spoke between segments.

"I've studied every protective charm that was ever placed on this scroll—the ones that weren't mine, I mean. Each charm requires a different spell to reverse or counteract it. The night we brought Daksh out of the Cascabela, I started removing them. For the final steps, I wanted witnesses.

"The most critical words aren't actually on the scroll, but bound just above the surface, floating in a sense. Each rune was enchanted in its place—movable in point of fact, so that the scroll could be jumbled at a moment's notice. This is one of the older protections the scroll has."

His wand swirled, and for several minutes a profusion of spells in a slew of different languages flowed out of his mouth. Perspiration was forming on his brow, and his hands were shaking. A slew of characters seemed to spill out of the scroll and onto the table before evaporating. He wiped his forehead with the back of his hand as he paused.

"The scroll must be opened to remove the rest of the charms, but neither the straps nor the scroll may be touched by human hands at this point—Karthika?"

She did not respond verbally, or even move—but the scroll lifted off the table, unbound its ties, and unrolled.

"A little more if you would, please. Yes, perfect. Flatten it out in the air, as if on a table. That is exactly what I needed, thank you."

The scroll now floated before us, quite stationary in the air. Spindlebrock breathed in deeply before continuing his litany of spells. Some he explained, while others were so dark that neither he nor anyone present wished to dwell on them. At one point, it seemed as if he was going to faint; Daksh and I rushed to his sides and supported him. The process was impossibly lengthy, it seemed, but did finally culminate in a definite end.

"This scroll is now little more than a piece of very old parchment, but even that cannot be allowed to remain. Karthika, can you help me, please? I want utter annihilation, and my energy is spent so that I need help to even stand."

I'm told that very few magicians can do what she did then. Telekinesis requires great spacial awareness, and a certain tangible closeness to the physical world; you have to know and feel and understand the way things are put together. I've heard that many artists have some amount of telekinesis. Spindlebrock later explained to me that she separated every fiber of the parchment, but that simple explanation doesn't convey the impression that was made: Imagine a scroll floating in midair, stretched taut and beyond, then suddenly exploding. But not in an explosion of chaos, with particles flying randomly in all directions; instead, imagine it bursting apart yet still floating and arranged as a scroll, the particles slowly separating until you could see through the spaces.

It was mesmerizing to watch. I was so fixated on the scroll that I didn't even notice the small container she had floated onto the table. The particles began to funnel themselves into it until they were spent, and the container sealed itself.

Chapter 26

Time to Settle

If there had been final goodbyes during that time I would have included them, but as it stands Sanjay, Karthika, and Daksh are still close and in regular contact (though, Daksh goes by another name now, and tends to avoid revealing his odd story to anyone). Speaking for Olivia and I, I believe I can accurately say that we left India not only having lived through some unique experiences, but also having made several new lifelong friends. We spent another two days with them while we arranged our trip home, then parted ways.

In many ways the trip was far more enlightening than we had initially anticipated. We gained context for understanding some of the manifestations that Olivia had studied for so long. We didn't really answer my questions about God with any degree of clarity; if anything, my questions only grew in complexity. Even so, contrasted with what we gained, I was hardly worried about what I had yet to uncover. My mind was already more full of new information than I could manage.

Our original return flight tickets were canceled, as Spindlebrock wanted us to join him on his private jet. He's a communicative man, who loves conversation when in the right mood—and for some reason, flying gets his mouth moving more than anything else. To be fair, I think he understood that Olivia and I must still have some things we wished to discuss, and that the thoughts would begin to flow more readily now that we were physically disconnecting from the situation—this is the way of the human mind; it needs time to settle. Our discussion on the way back to Toronto was filled with settling questions. As it was incredibly informative and memorable for me, it may be of value to you, reader. And so, I will attempt to include the most relevant parts here. I don't pretend that this is our whole conversation, and I can't say that this is the exact order or wording of it, but I've captured the essential information.

"I have to express a concern," he started once we were in the air and leveled off.

"As you might have imagined, I've pondered extensively over the years, on the concept of revealing my secret to others. There were encouragements from Karthika and Sanjay to destroy the scroll and live a normal life; that in and of itself is fine, but I don't know that they ever considered what it would mean to me personally if I revealed my position to anyone but them. I can't say that they never considered it, just that it wasn't ever brought up. I think they believed I would simply destroy the scroll, then live out my life and not reveal what had happened.

"When it was clear that you two were looking at studying ghosts, I started thinking harder about the possibility—I knew that if I was to have your help with Daksh, it would be difficult to keep the truth from you both. And then, of course, there was the matter of the scroll. The interplay between that recovery effort and the object itself also brought risk of exposure, and Lowen proved that the risk was in fact real."

"But, what was your concern?" inquired Olivia.

"Well, there were a few things, I think. My primary concern was losing friends. You might think that after so many years, I wouldn't care. Maybe I've promoted that perception—no, let's be clear: I have promoted it. Most definitely. But the truth is, I do care. You have no idea what it means to live as long as I have, with almost no real friends. There are so few people that I trust. I count you two among my best friends, though that may seem odd to you. I worried that we couldn't have a friendship, if you knew my past."

"Everyone makes mistakes. Real friends wouldn't abandon you because they found that you had made some," I offered.

"It's not just that—it's the awkwardness of it all. You're both observers of human behavior, you know how age gaps impact interpersonal interaction. I've spent most of my life being out of sync with humanity, and I've approached friendships and acquaintances on my own false terms. But I can't have false terms when my friends know the truth—and I don't want false terms any longer! I want real ones. But how can two young people like you be friends with an almost two hundred year old man?"

"We already thought you were two or three times our age," piped up Olivia. "What's the difference in a dozen decades or so more?"

The professor laughed heartily. It doesn't really seem strange given all that had happened, but he had a sort of lightness that I had never felt in him before—having let go of such a burden—and it was wonderful.

"And you feel the same way, Thomas? Do you both really not see any impediment to our friendship?"

Olivia shook her head, and I responded.

"I actually think this helps things. You were so far advanced in so many ways, it made you feel almost impossible to approach. Now we know how and why you have your attainments—it makes you more human, on multiple levels."

"I'm concerned about Delphine," he continued, his eyes distant. "She's not as young and mentally flexible as you two, I think, and she's been lied to enough in her life. I don't know how she'll take it, or if she'll forgive me—but it's a complication that I've created and that I must resolve."

He paused for a time. The plane banked slightly and we watched the ground rotate into view as we sat in silence.

"There is, of course, the matter of publicity. The Council will say nothing, and I trust that you two will keep this between us for now. I'm not sure when it will be needful or helpful to reveal all this—maybe I won't control that, I'm not certain."

(This was, of course, no longer a concern when I started in on these book projects, which are intended to clarify things that have already been revealed in other ways.)

"It's not our place to share the details of your private life."

"Thank you, Olivia. Privacy is important to me, but I want to clarify something: It's not my privacy that I'm thinking about just now. It's just that there are adjustments—reforms that I would like to initiate before this all comes to light. Once the truth about the scroll—and about me—is generally known, magicians in the commonality will take a different view of things. There will be concerns about the Council, about the safety of the commonality. Reality will change, at least perceptions of it—it could even impact beliefs. I want to be careful and cautious, not reckless and indifferent. Nothing about the scroll has been easy, that's for sure."

"You said earlier the scroll was passed down from magician to magician—and that Rognvald had actually figured it out to some degree?" I asked.

"That's true."

"But if he had figured it out, then why didn't the magicians—was the first one Matthias?"

"It was Mattis."

"Mattis—why didn't he and everyone after him, use the scroll to extend their lives? And why would they ever sell it?"

"Rognvald withheld portions of the spells for himself, and his apprentice Mattis didn't have any insights into those missing pieces. He knew that there was a solution to the problem, and he dedicated his life to finding it. So did many who followed after him, with some breakthroughs but never what you would call success. I think as time went on— hundreds of years, mind you—the entire endeavor faded in importance or perceived feasibility. Perhaps at some point, to one of the apprentices, fortune became more interesting than an endless pursuit of something that seemed impossible."

"But when did you get the scroll?"

"That part was easy. The scroll had already been sold multiple times before I purchased it; it was a matter of offering the right amount for it, that is all."

"What about the Pyre Reich?", Olivia asked. "You said they pursued the scroll originally. Why didn't they buy it?"

"Perhaps they did at some point, I have no way of knowing. Being obsessed with an end doesn't mean that you'll ever attain that end; if they ever had the scroll, they certainly didn't have the wherewithal to complete the research to put it to use. Or, perhaps they found easier ways —or maybe they really were just a mythology themselves. I have unanswered questions myself, about the Pyre Reich."

"And the scroll copy that's encapsulated in the foundation of the Cascabela, you're sure that can't be used?" I asked.

"One would have to dig up the casino to get to it; but for so great a prize I suppose that wouldn't matter. No, even if they went to that kind of trouble, the replica scroll doesn't contain any of the magic that was concentrated in the actual scroll, only some superficial information. You see, scrolls are similar to potions in a sense—they actually store magical power. The magic that you are able to perform with the help of a scroll would normally place far too high a demand on a person. This is the very reason scrolls were created.

"And, the original enchantments of the Rognvald Scroll are lost to time; I knew how to access the power, but I don't actually know the fine details of how the scroll was originally created. At this point, the copy of the scroll is interesting merely as a relic, but not as an object of power."

"Could you ever retrieve it, using the scroll case?"

"Without the corresponding real scroll? No, I'd have to dig it up. I may do that one day—not for the scroll, but for the case. I'd like to have both halves of that fascinating Selectivam Ostium in my possession. Though, it has to be properly placed in a confluence, just like the door that leads to the cave."

"I have a question about the cave," Olivia interjected. "Karthika said it was a 'good place for remembering.' What did she mean?"

"The cave is in a confluence, in a point where small fluctuations in the Strata Temporis and Strata Spatium join, as I showed you on the map. Not only can you use the Selectivam Ostium portal, there are other influences on space and time. In that particular location—due perhaps to the exact placement in the confluence, or some other features of the place—memory accessibility is impacted. I absolutely love to study there, actually, because I find that my studies are greatly enhanced."

Olivia and I must have been wide-eyed at this revelation. Spindlebrock laughed before continuing.

"You two look like kids in a candy store! We'll return there, don't worry, and to other places like it. I told you that I intended to make you both a part of my studies of the confluences. They are one of the magical facets of this world that fascinate me the most. You'll see the maps again, and more—it's my intention to make you both my apprentices, if you're willing."

Olivia and I were both appropriately stunned. Spindlebrock continued without taking any apparent notice.

"That's why I invented the reward for the return of Brevig's scroll—and I'm working on practicing my honesty here, so be patient with me. The reward was also a small sort of a test. I wanted to see how you would each react to the thought of obtaining a small fortune. It didn't sway either of you in the slightest, in terms of your personal convictions and goals. I am not shocked, knowing your characters, but I can't tell you how pleased it made me! There are far too many people who would sell their so-called convictions for a life of ease, and I'm of the opinion that they could never feel at ease with such a life as they imagine money could give them. All that said, you're still entitled to the promised reward, of course—and don't try to refuse, I've actually set up trustee accounts for you both. The money is already legally yours."

We transitioned from appropriately stunned to entirely dumbstruck. I attempted some fumbling, muttered refusal, but the professor cut it off.

"There's really nothing you can say—when I said apprentice, I meant it in the full sense, fortune included. This will change things for you. You may have envisioned lives centered somewhat around careers—now, you can devote yourselves to study and learning, if you choose. As my apprentices in magic and as wonderfully talented magicians in your own rights, we can work together not only to unlock deeper mysteries of the magical sciences, but also to change the way magicians think and view their world! My mind is racing with ideas, as it hasn't done since before I had the scroll. I think the knowledge that my life is now limited has given me a new passion, to finish the work of my life before the inevitable end. I never understood as much as I do now, all the costs that I have paid as a result of my pursuit of that scroll—I'm glad to be rid of it."

For a time—I'm not sure how long it was—our conversation died out, as we all silently contemplated the possible new future that had been unveiled. We talked about other things, but they are faded beyond recognition in my memory. I do, however, recall one more fragment of discussion that is worth sharing here.

"There's something that bothers me," I began. "The experience I had with Evalyn; it doesn't make much sense to me. I don't understand how it worked, how it happened— how can you go into someone else's soul?"

"This is a deep topic, Thomas, which will stray into darkness in the application you witnessed. I have some related knowledge, and many theories, but it is not my area of expertise. Strictly speaking, you weren't in Evalyn's soul, I believe."

"The woman there, she said I was in her soul."

"You were most definitely not in her soul, but perhaps she thought so."

"Then where was I, and what was going on?"

"Like many others, I view a human being as a composite. There's the physical, tangible body; the easiest part to understand, though we understand even that very poorly. There's another layer, or iteration, or level as Sanjay would call it—let's call it the soul or the spirit. This is the thing that you and Olivia were really in pursuit of, though you didn't know it, when you were chasing after ghosts—and that is why finding Daksh and discovering his reality will not be sufficient to satiate your minds on that point. This soul or spirit is the unseen force that represents the true person. Many believe that this force—or layer, phase, etc.—is unending, immortal, extant after death.

"The state that you entered was created by that woman you found there. It was formed in the mind—and by mind, I am speaking of the space that exists where the soul and the body meet, nominally located in the organ known as the brain, which I see as an interface between two very unique layers of existence in a single being. Not to get too esoteric, but these things are not simple.

"In short, that woman created that state within Evalyn's mind, and was occupying it. My theory is that because she created it—it was a thing created—your gift of Conexus enabled you to follow and join her there."

"But how? I've never been able to do anything like that with anyone else."

"True, but Evalyn isn't like anyone else—and your contact with her seems to lead to a combination of multiple magical phenomena, it's not just your gift in play. I think that in Bardo's, because Evalyn was conscious and in control of her physical body, her state or condition was shielded from your detection in a way; either that, or the woman you met was protecting it from your detection. Either way, it led to the unpleasant experience you had there. With Evalyn unconscious, things were different; she, or they, couldn't keep you out."

"You said that this woman created that state? How would she be able to do that, in someone else's mind?"

"I don't know exactly. The dark magic involved in such an arrangement is considered forbidden by most. Enslaving the human mind is a pursuit that only the worst magicians undertake; there are consequences, pains. I, personally, would certainly consider it forbidden, culturally speaking.

"Yet to some, rules or conventions are not a warning to be heeded, but a challenge for them to defy. One thing I do know is that Evalyn would have had to agree to the arrangement; this is not something that could have been forced upon her. To force such a thing would be impossible, in my professional estimation."

"Why would she do it? Why let someone else into your mind like that?"

"There may be inducements that we don't know about; promises or lies. It's possible that Evalyn is a victim in this arrangement. Probable, even."

I thought long and hard about what the professor was sharing.

"But, who is she, this woman I saw? You said you might know who she was. And, why was she doing it?"

"I did say that I had an idea only; and you said you might be able to identify her, given the chance."

"Yes."

"It may or may not come as a surprise to you, Thomas, but I believe this woman that you saw is directly connected to Lowen, possibly in more ways than one. In the next few weeks, hopefully, when the Council convenes, we'll perhaps be able to get more answers about that. My personal feeling is that we'll find the rabbit hole is much deeper than we anticipate."

Chapter 27

Epilogue

Before I offer my final thoughts on the resolution of the lost Rognvald Scroll, I wish to address an oversight or inattention that the reader may have felt in connection with the length of time between the publication of my first book, Professor Spindlebrock's Little Blue Book of Traveling Spells, and this volume. During that interim, a close and beloved friend of mine became deathly ill. I dedicated a great deal of time and energy to that person's healing—not that I felt that I could control the outcomes of that illness, but out of love for the person. The realities of the demands on my time that this elected position put me in, contributed greatly to the delay of this book. I could apologize, but I don't feel sorry for my choice; I therefore proffer only an explanation.

I readily confess that because my work on this volume partially coincided with the timeline of that illness, I began to truly understand why a person (such as a young Cyrus Spindlebrock) might pursue an object like the Rognvald Scroll. Our desire to keep the ones we love with us in this life is powerful. If you haven't had a similar experience or desire, then you may not fully understand, but I comfort myself in thinking that many of my readers will know what

I'm talking about, and therefore forgive the time it has taken for my books, which has been dictated by life and conscience.

There was a promise, at the end of the first volume, of sharing three distinct and significant mysteries relating to W.C. Crane. This volume represents the second mystery. As quickly as I'm able, I will provide the reader with my recounting of the finale to the intrigues surrounding Crane, who you now know to be Lowen Walker, the famous entertainment tycoon (famous for those readers who are part of the magical commonality, at least). I have no desire to be coy; as I stated at the end of the first volume, Crane's story has a not-unpleasant ending. By this, I mean to reveal that Lowen Walker did not turn out to be a monstrous villain, as at least I supposed when I was first thrust into the mystery of his abductions. He was a person who made mistakes, as we all are. Worse than most, it is true—but, he owned up to those mistakes, and though less dramatic in the view of some, such an ending is worth sharing and worth reading about. As to the mystery that is entangled with the close of his story, it has enough of the dramatic on its own to satisfy. I look forward to explaining it more fully.

As for the final resolution of the Rognvald Scroll, to say that it was reduced to dust is really only a partial answer. If I were to inform you that said dust was later dispersed over Lake Ontario, you still would not have the full story. The view that gives the most complete perspective is one that looks at over a thousand years of magical and scientific history, and examines the hearts of each person involved. There are many reasons to desire control over the extent of our mortal lives; greed and covetousness being perhaps the most common. But not all who erred in this history were evil, it seems to me. As with all history, the bare facts, stories, legends, and mythologies aren't sufficient tools to arrive at a judgment. Who can sound the depths of the heart, with such feeble tools?

For me, the real story of the lost Rognvald Scroll lies not in its theft and recovery, nor in the fact of its destruction; more important than all of these are the mistakes that were absolved, the truths that were revealed, and the lives that were freed. The magical world is now in possession of the whole story, which can crush (if you'll let it) rumor, gossip, fabrication, and lie; the non-magical reader may not understand just what this means, nor where this is all leading—but in the next and final volume, all will be revealed.

Joseph D. Lyman

I've loved writing since before I understood what the wavy letters I was scrawling even meant. As a young man, I wanted to create fiction—and as an adult, I've learned that there is nothing stopping me.

This book, like those I have written and will write, represents the ideas, plots, places, characters, and situations that I find most interesting. Whether they will interest the reader is another question altogether; I hope that they will, but I can't control the universe.

This series is a start for me, an experiment in the process of writing. Research can only take a person so far. Eventually, we have to step into the wide and dark expanse of the unknown, to see where our feet will lead us. With the years I have left, I hope to not only finish this series, but also to embark on countless new adventures. It is my sincere hope that you will share those with me.